CENTRAL CITY

INDY PERRO

Indy Perro is a novelist, an independent thinker, and a recovering academic. Indy has a degree in history, graduate degrees in religious studies, comparative literature, and education, and has spent more than a decade teaching philosophy, religious studies, writing, and literature. Indy speaks and reads English, Spanish, and French, and his German improves most days.

Please visit Indy's website Indyperro.com

CENTRAL CITY

—————

Indy Perro

DOG'S NAME PRESS

First edition published in 2020 by
🐕 Dog's Name Press
PO Box 276
Niwot, CO 80544

ISBN 978-1-952258-00-8
Library of Congress Control Number: 2020935191

Book Design by Brizida Magro

Everything for A.S.S.
You bet your...

PROLOGUE

February 12, 1977

THE MAN'S SHADOW spread across the snow, tinted gold by porchlight.

He pulled his keys from his pocket, fumbled with them, dropped them into the snow next to the stoop, picked them up, shook them off, and shoved the correct key into the lock. The door creaked on its hinges and slammed into the frame with a high-pitched smack.

The crisp, cold air from outside stressed the smell of fried butter and boiled milk, leftover mac and cheese, and scrambled eggs still crusted on pot and pan. The man, entranced by the living room, leaned against the door, conserving his strength. Frayed paper ornaments, the remnants of a family project years before, decorated a plastic Christmas tree that sat in darkness next to the cold television, a makeshift parent and babysitter. A calendar, fourteen months behind schedule, claimed it was still December.

The naked bulb in the entryway clicked and buzzed, and the man stepped forward, stumbling into the coat rack and falling to the floor in a pile of cotton, wool, polyester, and nylon. He pushed himself to his knees, grabbed the rack, set it upright, and used it to steady himself. For a few beats, the man and the rack rocked to the rhythm of the man's breathing.

He released his reluctant partner, dropped to one knee, and began to sort the coats and hang them by their collars. He picked up his youngest son's and mumbled to himself.

"This one cost a pretty penny."

The man held the jacket into the light and looked at the dried blood streaking down the front and along the right sleeve. The man dabbed at the brown stains. He turned the coat over and felt the tear below the arm, black-and-white feathers floating from his fingers.

"Adam. Get your ass down here."

The boy, waiting and watching, stepped out of the shadows at the top of the stairs. "Yes, sir."

"What the hell is this?"

"That's my new coat."

"I know what it is. I bought the damn thing. What is this shit here?" The man waved the coat, bunched in his fist, toward the stairs.

"Blood."

"I know what dried blood looks like. I've seen enough in my time."

The man threw the coat at his son, and its arms fanned out in flight, gliding the garment to the stairs, not quite halfway to the top. Three feathers listed in the coat's wake.

The man stumbled forward and braced himself on the railing near the bottom step. "What the hell is blood doing on it?"

The older brother spoke from the doorway of their shared room. "It wasn't his fault. Some kids were picking on him. I took care of it."

"You stay out of this, boy. You didn't take care of shit. This little bastard ruined his new coat."

The older brother stepped to the top of the stairs and pushed his younger brother behind him, and the man, finding his balance, took the stairs two at a time.

Four photographs in matching white oak frames hung on the wall along the staircase. One showed the two brothers, laughing in an embrace, on the hood of a squad car one sunny summer afternoon. Another, a black-and-white image of potential bliss, showed the man and a woman at the altar on their wedding day. The woman looked like the younger boy, short and solid, fair-skinned with blond hair, and a dimple in the right cheek. The third photograph showed the entire family in a photographer's studio, clearly posed in front of a woodland backdrop, their expressions captured between irritability and the word cheese.

The final photograph showed the woman standing next to an easel with a painting of a little brown dog running toward a cabin through a swaying field of tall grass, not the work of a professional. The lines wavered, and the perspective tilted, bunching the cabin to one side, but the colors, like the woman, caught the eye.

The woman wore a veteran's association t-shirt stained with seven colors of paint, and she laughed into the camera, a happiness larger than life, with just the faintest yellowing on the outer edge of her left eye. The same painting hung obscured by the tree in the living room downstairs.

When the man reached the top of the stairs, the distance between the last step and the top nullified the three inches of height that differentiated father and son. The two shared the same coloring, the same eyes, the same smile, and, in that moment, the same squint and tightened jaw.

"When I was a kid, we didn't get new clothes. Do you know what I've done to provide for you? Do you know?"

The older brother turned away from the sour smell of stale liquor.

The backhand rolled the older boy off his feet and into the hall.

The man towered over the youngest. "You're just like your mother. You don't know what you got, what you want. You think I'm made of money. You think everything's about you."

The blows knocked the boy to the floor and kept coming. The man stood over him, held him down with his knee, and used both hands. Fury so blinded the man he never saw the older boy's fist, but the strike to the temple knocked him into the rail at the top of the stairs and his drunken disequilibrium toppled him downward. The man half-slid and half-rolled. The tools of his trade jutting from his belt caught and slowed his descent. The light from the entryway flickered off the shield, bronze against the navy-blue uniform.

The older boy turned his brother to look at his face. The younger boy opened his eyes. "This ain't nothing, kid. You might look a little tough for a while, but you'll live."

The boy's eyes turned away from his older brother and looked into the darkness beyond. The nightstick caught the older boy between the elbow and the shoulder of his right arm, and the bone popped.

He cried out, fell to the left, and held his arm close to his body as he slid away from his father, inching down the hall.

The father pointed the club at his oldest son. "You're next."

The younger boy covered his head with his hands and tucked his knees into his chest.

After the fifth strike of the club, the older brother screamed, "You're going to kill him. He's just a kid."

The man didn't seem to notice. He kept swinging and swinging, his eyes glazed over, and saliva collected at the corners of his mouth.

The younger boy's hands reached out to his father, trying to stop the blows, fumbling with the objects on his belt.

The older boy pushed himself to his feet with his good arm and threw himself into the man, reaching for a weapon. The pain on his right side pierced his brain, and he never heard the shot.

The man slumped against the railing, his head tucked into his chest, and his arms, nightstick in one hand, lay lifeless at his sides. Neither boy moved, consciousness lost beneath the blows, and if it weren't for the pool of blood growing beneath the man, they may all three have simply slept.

Frozen and framed within the fourth photograph, the woman watched through eyes squinted in laughter, head tilted back, silent.

ONE

———

A CASE OF THE JITTERS
8:12AM Tuesday, September 1, 1992

Nothing Detective Bayonne had seen during his twenty-three years on the force prepared him for this homicide.

A lot of things can throw a detective. A guy walks into a crime scene unprepared for the brutality pounded into the corpse, the fear spread across the floor, the hatred sprayed across a mirror, or the passion sliced off and tossed in the corner. After a while, though, a detective gets used to it. He learns to turn the volume down on his emotions and listen, hear what he needs to hear. Bayonne had taken this to the extreme. In his mind, most cases busted at the seams with something to say. They wanted to talk. A good detective, and Bayonne considered himself one, knew, within five minutes, why a murder was committed.

That doesn't get the job done.

That only gets it started.

It might've been the butler or Miss Scarlet in the library with the candlestick, but a good detective stands in the library, examines the blood on the paperbacks, and knows from experience what it looks like and what it means when somebody uses a candlestick to collapse a cranium. Bayonne's job, as he understood it, was to find out where the butler was and what Miss Scarlet thought of the victim.

Murder leaps on a soap box and preaches desire, anger, perversion, or any combination of the three. Even professional jobs look like they were done by dispassionate professionals. On occasion, and this is rare, some mastermind who thinks he knows how clever he is tries to disguise what he did. These rocket surgeons watch television like everybody else, so they know their business. Well, Dr. Moriarty must've gotten his degree out of a Cracker Jack box, because the physical evidence never lies. The cuts don't fall at the right angle. The blow occurred after death. The blood splatter tells a different story, a story of a heart past pumping. The television gets it all wrong. Supermodels doing DNA tests rarely solve crimes. Cases close because experienced detectives read a scene, read the evidence, and understand forensics.

What threw Bayonne in this case, what kept this one just out of reach, was that it didn't preach. It didn't explain anything at all. He stood over the body and felt alone. Silence. He felt no murderer at all.

Bayonne might've been a little off that morning. He

hadn't slept well, and it was his first day with a new partner, a rookie detective fresh off the beat. The rookie should've cut his teeth on something simple, something where the wife or husband did it, where the answers were obvious, routine, and gave a sense of the reality of the job and, for that matter, maybe an honest lesson about life. Unfortunately, the sorry bastard landed an oddball as a partner and a curveball for a first case.

Bayonne didn't think Adam McKenna was a bad kid. Earnest and eager, two good qualities in a neophyte, even if they won't do anything for you on the job. Still, McKenna didn't look like much of a cop. He stood about five ten and had clearly gone to seed in the five years since he got out of the academy. Forty pounds overweight, he wore thick, horn-rimmed glasses and had platinum-blond hair buzzed short, almost invisible. His suit, a size too big to hide his girth, looked like he'd taken out a loan for it without realizing it would be stained by vomit or blood or both by the end of the week.

Bayonne wondered if McKenna would feel more comfortable in front of a computer than at a crime scene, and, in a moment of optimism, hoped he'd shoulder more than his share of the paperwork.

McKenna had the highest score on the detective's exam that Bayonne had ever seen, so the kid might not have been a total idiot. Some thought him a bit pompous, but Bayonne wasn't one to judge a college boy who doesn't know a muskox from a water buffalo. He'd been without a partner ten months, since his partner of twenty years transferred to a desk job downtown, the lucky bastard. Bayonne would've ridden with Barney Fife if he'd take a turn writing reports.

Bayonne pushed *Houses of the Holy* into the tape deck, cranked the knob to discourage conversation, and he and Adam drove out of St. Patrick's precinct garage and turned right, heading south on 40th Ave.

Between Jefferson Street and the Lincoln Cemetery, all the houses were built either before the Depression or in the '50s.

Originally, the neighborhood had been an Irish settlement that housed dockworkers and unskilled labor for the south side packing plants and factories. During the Depression, many of the factories closed and the city fell on hard times. Workers who kept their jobs moved closer to the factories and into cheaper tenements below South Street.

After the war, young professionals built new houses in the old neighborhood and started families. Their kids went to college and moved downtown or uptown for work before moving north or out to the suburbs to raise the next generation. By the late '70s, St. Patrick's was a working-class neighborhood again, with what remained of the older, Irish families seasoned by the arrival of later migrants.

As they drove by the Lincoln Cemetery, with its hundred and fifty-year-old mausoleums housing generations of politicians, barons of industry, Benedictines, and Jesuits, and its smaller, less conspicuous internments, Bayonne's mind drifted to the cops he'd seen laid to rest there. A couple young guys and an old veteran who'd made a rookie mistake. They'd been friends, in a way, guys he'd had a drink with from time to time. The old guy's son was his dentist, and one young guy's widow lived in his neighborhood. She wasn't that young anymore. She'd moved on, had a new family. How long had it been since her husband died? Ten years? Maybe fourteen? Bayonne didn't know.

Lost in his thoughts, he'd forgotten he had a partner. Adam had turned down "D'Yer Mak'er" and was saying something. Bayonne had to clear his head to register Adam's words.

". . . you know what I'm saying?"

"What are you saying?"

"Well, what are we going to find here?"

"A dead person. That's our job."

"I mean, I've worked cases on patrol, but I was always guarding a perimeter or canvassing."

There wasn't really a question there, and Bayonne didn't know what to say. He didn't want to be a jerk, but he didn't want to make his young partner's life too easy, either. This kid was green, and it wouldn't do him any good to tell him what he needed to see. Adam would either figure it out or he wouldn't.

Bayonne turned right on Arapahoe, and said, "You'll do fine. Just watch and listen. Don't try to do too much. I'll tell you if you need to do something you aren't doing. Otherwise, just take a deep breath, take everything in, and do your best to learn."

Bayonne turned into an alley and parked at an angle behind a small house he'd driven by a hundred times, a cookhouse that served as a flop for prostitutes and junkies. It was an eyesore with paint flaking off the front and a couch sitting in the yard, rotting, foam poking out of the tears in the fabric. Two patrolmen leaned against the back porch.

Bayonne cut the engine. "I hear you went to college."

Adam didn't say anything.

"That won't help you today. I know you learned a lot of good stuff there, and it will help in the long run. You'll be a better detective because of every book you've read, every little snippet you know about the world. But today"—Bayonne waved his hands, palms down, in a circle in the air between his chest and the steering wheel—"today, you need to stay here. Stay where you know what you're doing. Don't overextend, and let the game come to you. Take it one step at a time, and you'll begin to see where you need to step next."

Adam stared at Bayonne a few beats before saying, "Okay."

Bayonne nodded, slapped him on the arm, and stepped out of the car. Outside, Bayonne took a deep breath, pulled the tin out of his back pocket, and tapped it between his thumb and forefinger. Bayonne hated telling people their business, but he was a senior detective now. Part of his duty was to train the new litter of pups. He didn't feel that old, but he would by the end of the day. He pressed a wad into his lip, sucked on it a little, and spit a string of brown liquid onto the ground.

Adam walked around to Bayonne's side of the car. "I thought you smoked?"

"When you can't smoke, chew on this."

Bayonne took a step toward the house. Adam spoke from behind him. "You know I've been a cop for five years."

"You've been a detective thirty minutes."

Adam didn't respond, so Bayonne walked toward the house. Crumpled beer cans stood out among the cigarette butts that littered the back yard, grass tan and dying with the shortening days of summer and the arrival of crisp winds that penetrate to midday. The occasional glass shard or bent syringe gave the debris field a tougher, more delinquent appearance.

Bayonne tipped his hat to the two patrolmen, both of whom acknowledged him by name and nodded to his partner. Two men and a woman sat in plastic chairs around a plastic table on the concrete slab behind the house. None made eye contact, and Bayonne didn't stop to talk.

He led the way into the lime-green kitchen, linoleum peeled and cracked, wallpaper stained brown where it wasn't stripped off by idle hands fueled by synthetic energy, a pile of dirty dishes in the sink, and a stack of pizza boxes in a corner. Sauce pans with brown residue sat on the gas stove.

The kitchen opened onto a living room with two faded, stained, and torn flower-print couches and a lawn chair facing a television on the floor. An ashtray overflowed next to a disheveled Monopoly board, a half dozen cans, and an empty plastic handle on a coffee table constructed of a sheet of plywood balanced on two cardboard boxes. Pink, green, and yellow money had rained on the party. Empty beer cans had been crunched and stashed throughout the room, and a portable cassette player with a cracked face lay on its back next to the television. Bayonne didn't look for anyone's lost shaker of salt.

A hallway branched to the left, three doors, all ajar. Bayonne called down the hall, "You here, Doc?"

"First room on the left, Bayonne."

With his partner nipping at his heels, Bayonne took the time to glance in the other two rooms. The bedroom had two single beds, dirty sheets drooped toward the floor, no pillows. The bathroom had a rusty sink covered in hair and dried toothpaste. Someone had dropped a chunky deuce in the toilet.

Bayonne stepped into the crime scene and stood next to the crouched medical examiner.

"Enjoy the nickel tour?" the ME asked.

"No."

The man on the floor, sporting his birthday suit, had curled into the fetal position, his hands folded in a prayer that died on his lips, which were opened in a final, silent, and passive gasp. A puddle of brown, mostly liquid, had leaked from his anus and spread toward the bed. Bayonne slipped on rubber gloves and crouched close to the body. Beneath the emanation of feces hung the fragrance of dried sweat, the stale, bitter aroma of nicotine and old smoke, and the metallic odor of cocaine mixed with baking soda.

Bayonne sat on his ankles and used a pen to raise the corpse's top hand. "What's the story?"

"He's been dead maybe three or four hours, maybe longer. He died right here, on the floor. He might've overdosed, but there is some bruising here on the neck that looks like it matches the belt there with his clothes. His belt, I think. There was no struggle, but I believe the hands have been posed this way."

"No struggle?"

"Maybe he knew the killer. Maybe there was no killer. Maybe they were in here together, getting high. Judging by the track marks, he was almost certainly high when he died, though we'll know more about that in a few days. He could've been into erotic asphyxiation. I honestly don't know. If somebody strangled him, they used a light touch, which is pretty unusual for murder. If he'd been passed out at the time, it wouldn't have taken much."

"Could it have been a woman?"

"Maybe a woman. Maybe a guy who was as faded as his buddy, didn't know what he was doing. Maybe an accident. Maybe an overdose."

"Jesus, that's a lot of maybes."

The doctor straightened up and let out a long sigh.

"And you're sure there was no struggle?"

"I see no definitive signs of an attack or battle. The bruises on the arms are old, most are extensions of the track marks, and the marks on the wrist came from posing the hands, I think."

"Is he praying? Asking forgiveness?"

"I assemble the facts, Bayonne. It's your job to interpret them."

He had a point. "Could someone other than the killer have posed the hands?"

"It's possible, but unlikely. It was done within a few minutes of expiration, moments, really."

Bayonne glanced at the rumpled sheets. "I'm interested to see if he'd been drugged. Also, be sure to have forensics check the sheets for semen."

"Routine stuff, but in a place like this, we're going to find semen by the gallon."

Bayonne pointed to where the wood around the lock had been cracked, forced open, and his partner's eyes followed his gesture.

"The door was kicked in. Did you find debris on the body?"

"Yeah. It had been kicked in after the murder. Somebody locked the body in here, and whichever of those jokers outside found the body kicked the door in to do it."

The doctor wiped his brow with the back of his wrist, above the rubber glove. He stepped aside and began to examine the nightstand and bed, giving Bayonne's partner his first clear view of the victim.

Adam collided with the wall on his way outside.

"This your partner's first case?"

"Enjoying his promotion."

The doctor never looked up from his work. "It's probably the responsibility more than the sight of the dead man.

I'm sure he's seen bodies on patrol, but knowing he's been charged with solving this case, that can be a heavy burden."

"Tell me about it."

Bayonne left the doctor to collect his data and moved through the house assembling his theory, or what passed for a theory, no clear motive or sequence of events, only possibilities. In the kitchen, Bayonne paused and took a snort from the flask he kept in his jacket.

Outside, an older patrolman, fifty pounds overweight and twenty years past a possible promotion, pulled a moist towelette out of a package as he spoke to Adam. "The job gets to us all now and again. I remember this one time, in Commerce City, I saw—"

One of the men on the porch giggled.

Bayonne turned to the porch and locked eyes with the other patrolman, who'd been an Army Ranger in the Gulf War. Bayonne and the former Ranger kept their expressions blank.

The giggler wore a tailored suit, rumpled from a long night. His hair had been disheveled from nocturnal activities or gale force winds, and its rise from his scalp exposed a timely recession.

Cindy Doyle sat next to him, a woman of the night who worked out of a couple different clubs in St. Patrick's and Commerce City. She wore a skintight Salvation Army cocktail dress beneath a black hoodie. Her fingers tugged at the snot-stained cuffs.

And finally, there was Jimmy Mason, a short, fat, slob of a man who knew his business, how to mind it, and how to keep his mouth shut, but not much else. Mason worked for Peter Di Vittorio and ran the house, and the connection to Petey V, Bayonne assumed, was the reason Bayonne had gotten the case.

Bayonne spit a string of juice and took a deep breath, happy not to have to gut the stuff for a while, and nodded for Mason to step into the yard with him.

"We don't want no trouble here. We don't know whose name's on the lease. I found the body in the room there, like I told you guys over the phone."

Bayonne had figured as much. Nobody else would've kicked in the door unless they'd been smashed, which somebody might've been, but they weren't here now.

"How much did you clean up?"

"Nothing in that room. I swear." Mason paused and glanced over Bayonne's shoulder where Adam had approached, cleaning his lips with a baby wipe.

"My new partner, Detective McKenna."

Mason nodded toward Adam and looked into Bayonne's eyes. The detective nodded. "We cleaned up a few things in the kitchen, you know. We didn't want to cause you guys too much trouble. Look, it's an overdose. Mikey was hitting it pretty hard last night. I think he forgot to measure or lost track or something."

"What was the victim's full name?"

"Michael Connolly."

"Where did he live?"

"I don't know, somewhere on the south side. Either St. Patrick's or just over into SOCCs. He was a bartender over at Alfie's. He came over here after work. That's all I know. He was a good guy, but reckless. You know? He couldn't always handle his high."

Bayonne nodded, told Mason he'd take care of things, and sent Mason on his way. Mason glanced over Bayonne's shoulder again, at the other two. Mason wanted to stick around, to be sure everybody knew what to say. Bayonne smiled and jerked his finger toward the heel-toe expressway.

Bayonne called the giggler over and asked him if he lived there. He watched Mason's Pontiac disappear down the street before answering.

"No, sir. Just visiting friends."

Bayonne examined the guy's identification before giving him a closer look. Beneath his tailored britches, Bernie Peters was thirty-eight going on late fifties, pink skin tones with blotchy patches of broken blood vessels. He stood with a slight lean, like he'd just run a marathon, and when he fished a cigarette out of a crumpled soft pack, he sucked on it like it contained salvation. Bayonne could see the clarity in his eyes fading as they grew more bloodshot. Bayonne tallied his wardrobe, and the shoes, crimson wingtips, put him well over a grand, and the guy had straight, white teeth, which was rare enough among sober people in that part of town.

"What are you doing in this neighborhood?"

Bernie smiled at Bayonne before answering, like he knew Bayonne wouldn't do anything to him. Mason had connections, which afforded him a lot of latitude if he didn't cross a line, but Mason was worried. Mason knew juice needed to be strained. This guy thought he knew something else, something he'd always felt, something only money can teach you, which begged the question, why was he still here?

"Like I said, just visiting friends. Mason found the body. I waited around just to give a statement, but I don't have much to say. I didn't see anything, didn't even know the guy before last night."

At the time, Bayonne thought him the most pathetic brand of asshole, a tourist, someone who trolled the far side of the tracks for shits and giggles. Bayonne assumed he'd never seen death before and the danger gave him a thrill.

Adam wrote down his name and address, a house in The Heights, and Bayonne sent him on his way. Bayonne spit out the wad in his lip and gave his partner a good once-over. It was a chilly day, but perspiration gathered at the young man's hairline.

"You hanging in there?"

"I'm fine."

"You don't look fine. Haven't you seen a dead body before?"

"It's not that."

"What is it then?"

"I don't know." Adam hadn't looked Bayonne in the eye once during the entire conversation. "There was something about the way he looked, the belt marks on his neck, and the way his hands were posed. It made me think of something."

"What?"

"I don't know. Something I've seen somewhere."

"Something you saw on patrol? At a crime scene?"

"No. Nothing like that. Something a long time ago, when I was a kid. I'm not sure where I was or if it actually happened."

"You want a smoke?"

Adam shook his head.

"It might help you lose weight."

Adam didn't say anything, so Bayonne led the way over to Cindy Doyle. Bayonne sat next to her, offered her a cigarette, lit it, and lit his own. He doubted they inhaled any salvation, but Cindy's hand stopped shaking.

"How you been, Cin?"

"I get by. I haven't seen you around in a while."

"What were you doing here?"

"Me and Diamond were staying here."

Bayonne knew Diamond Molloy, another pro. "Were you two living here?"

"Not living, really, just staying here the last couple of nights. Mason was helping us out. You know, getting us high."

Bayonne did know. He knew Diamond had taken a turn, and he was sorry to see Cindy following her down the rabbit hole. "Where have you been working lately?"

The girl shrugged again. "You know, around. The Saddle mostly." Her pupils were the size of silver dollars.

"Did Jimmy Mason have you working his customers?"

"Sometimes. He paid us a little, but mostly we got a place to crash and a free touch when we needed it." She ran her hand under her nose and snorted, pulling the snot back into her sinuses, at least for the moment. When it flowed, it came in a torrent. "We came from work, and we'd been partying all night. You know? People were here and gone. There were maybe twenty people in and out of the house all night. A bunch of us had been playing Monopoly, Mikey, too. Some other girls came over, friends of mine and Diamond's. We all split up for a while, you know? I hung with Mason in the kitchen while he was working. We smoked a little, had a few laughs. People took off. We never got back to the Monopoly game. I hadn't seen Mikey in a while and went to check on him this morning, and the door was locked."

"Did you kick it in?"

"Mason did. I made him do it. I was worried. I knew Mikey had been pretty high. You never know what can happen. But when the door opened, there he was, dead like that. Diamond, Cassandra, and Molly Matches were still here then, but they split when they heard what happened. Mason said we had to stay. He said he couldn't fix it. He called you."

"I need the names of everyone who was here last night."

Cindy took Bayonne's notepad and began to scribble.

Bayonne stared at the puke splash on his partner's shoes, shook his head, and looked at the side of the mouse's face. There was something else, something nobody was saying.

Bayonne didn't really know Cindy Doyle. He'd bumped

into her at the bars around the neighborhood, and women in her line of work always made an effort when rubbing elbows with a cop, especially if the cop didn't try to push or ask for anything. Bayonne thought he was one of the good ones, but he realized, perhaps for the first time, that Cindy, in her own way, was one of the good ones, too. Cindy cared about the people around her. She wasn't just a piece of the puzzle disarrayed before him. She wasn't a party girl, at least not anymore. She was a woman past her prime, a hard-lived forty, cracks showing on her forehead, cheeks, at the edges of her eyes, and on the backs of her hands. Her blood had thinned, and her mind frayed by the only life she'd ever known. She cared about this case more than he did. She'd liked Michael Connolly. She'd lost a friend.

Bayonne took a deep breath, his consciousness piqued by his realization, and when he spoke, he spoke to Cindy's softer side. He reached toward her, hoping she'd reach back toward him. "What do you think happened, Cindy?"

"What everybody thinks, I guess. He overdosed. He wasn't a very bright guy, you know, and he was lit last night. He was drunk before he even got here."

"Did Mason take the belt off his neck?"

Her eyelid flickered. "What belt?"

Bayonne sucked on the nail and flicked ash into the yard.

She looked away. "Mason didn't want you to know about that. He told me not to tell you. He said you would think it was a murder, but that it was an accident."

"Did he like to be choked or strangled?"

"He never did any of that with me. He was a good guy, had a big heart. You know?"

Bayonne waited a beat before patting her on the knee and giving her his card and his best smile. "Thanks, girl. This stays between us. We won't give you a hard time. Let me know if you think of anything else."

When the hooker stood, she dropped her butt and used her platform heel to grind it into the concrete. She tucked Bayonne's card into the belly pouch of her hoodie and blew a cloud of smoke out of the side of her mouth.

"It's good seeing you, Vinnie. I could use a hard time after the night I've had."

Bayonne said, "So you know, we're going to play it like it lays. You can pass that along."

"If you really know how it lays, you're already fucked." She smiled, showed Bayonne her backside, and clacked toward the curb.

TWO

DIAL M
12:29AM Wednesday, September 2, 1992

A wooden and weathered sign faced the street, at eye level, to the right of The Taproom entrance. "On the other side of this door, your problems will still be your problems."

Kane Kulpa had laughed the first time he'd read that. He'd stopped laughing. He knew how true it was, and on the other side of the door, his problems would force him into a conversation he didn't know how to have.

The most difficult conversations are often the ones people don't have, the ones a person can't have because she, or in this case he, won't face the things inside himself that he despises, the things that make him squirm.

The ants in his pants that make him dance.

In the years after his father's death, Kane didn't have time to think about how much of his father had survived inside himself. The rage and the fear, Kane thought, were echoes of the tragedies he'd experienced. He'd been doing his best to survive and trying to be a man when he was still only a kid. Survival's not for the squeamish, and when a person is busy trying to survive, he doesn't have time to learn to appreciate beauty, to embrace a concept like faith, or, sometimes, even to maintain dignity.

Kane didn't think he was defining himself in the moments when he chose to fight, to push back against a fate holding him down. He thought he'd be able to change course once he entered an even field of play, once things leveled off.

Things don't level off.

In prison, he'd had plenty of time to think. He'd had time to read all the books he'd heard about in college but never read. In prison, he'd learned what shapes a man, how he becomes, through all the little moments he assumes inconsequential, the man he's going to become. He'd seen, first hand, the slow change that creeps into the features, the dead eyes, cold expressions, and scar tissue of the strong, or the ticks, confusion, jitters, compulsions, and muscle gone to flab of the weak. He'd learned to see beauty in the moments when he resisted pain. He'd learned to hold his faith as a shield against life's inquisitions, and he'd learned that dignity grows from the ability to accept loss, to understand the costs of different choices.

He'd been out of prison for more than six years the day he and Bruno Pantagglia walked into The Taproom to meet Tran Van Kahn.

Bruno, a short, round man with a head as bald as a billiard cue and hands the size of catcher's mitts that swung at his knees, tipped his right shoulder when he entered the bar. The movement gave the appearance that he burst into a room, and the eyes that turned his way saw a guerilla silhouetted in the doorway.

Tom, the bartender, nodded when they entered and mixed Bruno a gin and tonic and handed Kane a Newcastle.

Tom said, "Pete's waiting in his office."

Tom did for Pete what Kane did for Bruno. He maintained the bar, the books, the business, and Pete's general well-being.

Bruno and Kane carried their drinks through the maze of tables in the barroom. A few locals played a game of pool, and two working girls chatted at a table next to a group of guys who spoke with outside voices and wore stained jeans and denim shirts with names scrawled across iron-on patches, like they'd come straight from a construction site, started drinking around six, and their night had begun its inevitable descent.

Pete sat in his office at a table set for six and watched the three black-and-white video screens mounted in the armoire along the wall that doubled as a bar.

One camera hung inside a sconce above the front door, one was hidden in a speaker on the rear wall of the barroom, and another was hidden in a box on the top shelf of the bar. Pete wasn't worried about petty theft or robbery. No one would be that stupid. Pete liked information, and he'd been watching and waiting for the meeting to unfold.

He gestured for Bruno and Kane to sit, and when they did, he put his hand on Bruno's shoulder and nodded to Kane. A thin man with a long face, Pete looked to be a dash to Bruno's dot.

"There going to be trouble with Tran?" Bruno asked.

Peter Di Vittorio had never married. After his mother died, Bruno had been the closest thing to family he had. Neither were that old, only early fifties, but liver spots covered Pete's gaunt face. He raised the highball glass, three quarters full of Burgundy, to his lips and drained a third of the liquid. His weathered hand had developed a slight tremor. Kane had never seen him without a glass of wine. He sipped from a tumbler during the daylight hours and a tall glass after five.

To Kane's surprise, Petey V asked, "What do you think, Kane? Are we going to have trouble?"

Kane stared into those pale blue eyes for a few ticks. "That's up to you."

Pete made a clicking sound with his cheek and turned away.

Bruno cleared his throat. "I'm too old to fight a war, but if that's what you want to do, Pete . . .."

When Kane and Bruno had met nine years ago in jail, while Kane waited for his trial to begin, Kane had saved Bruno's life.

Bruno spent a month or two in the sling every other year or so. Whenever the cops needed to stack their numbers, they raided one of Bruno's places, which he technically owned even if they weren't all his. He was never present for the raids, always heard about them a day or two in advance, but rather than let someone else take the fall, he'd make a plea bargain for some petty nonsense and spend a few weeks as a guest of the city. He called it his vacation. Bruno had a busty Italian wife and seven kids. From what Kane had seen, Bruno was a pretty good husband and father, at least for a guy who ran drugs, a book, backroom poker games, and whorehouses. But seven kids were seven kids, and every time Kane had been to Bruno's house, a remodeled ranch style on Eighth Avenue, the place had been a bit chaotic. Bruno's youngest had recently turned eighteen, a senior in high school, but his four eldest all had children of their own, all lived within a few blocks, and all used grandma for daycare.

Kane believed he'd ignore the church after the fourth monster, but who was going to argue when the white hat had framed pride of place overlooking the dining room table? Bruno needed a vacation now and again, and his wife trusted him to stay out of trouble if he was already in trouble.

Bruno kept to himself in the hoosegow. Kane slept two beds over from the guy for two weeks, and Bruno hadn't said word one. Kane got the message Bruno's second day when Kane asked him if they could watch basketball instead of Jeopardy. Bruno didn't even glance in Kane's direction, but a fella named Mark, who'd been popped for soliciting an undercover cop, shook his head, so Kane sat back and tried to come up with a question for "Before and After" for four hundred.

Two weeks later, they were working their shift in the recycling center, and a guy of ambiguous ethnicity came up behind Bruno. Kane saw the guy had something in his hand and called out. Bruno turned just in time and got a good scrape rather than a second bellybutton. Bruno knocked the guy out and spent a week in the hospital, probably eating ice cream and getting sponge baths from cute nurses. When he made his way back to their wing of orange-clad nonviolent offenders, he gave Kane a warmer smile than he'd seen on Bruno's face since. The big lug actually shook Kane's hand. Bruno wasn't a bad guy when you got to know him. Kane just never knew anybody who knew him.

Bruno said one word, the only word Kane had heard out of him and the only one Kane was going to hear until Bruno's last day in the sling.

"Thanks."

Kane realized something as he watched the baby-faced knuckle-dragger gather his linens before his release. Bruno had been using sheets from home, and the guards had brought him books and bags of Cherry NIBS, his favorite candy. He'd been charged with racketeering and pandering, but the pandering had been tossed and the racketeering charges had been reduced to misdemeanors. He'd also been assessed fines for several zoning and health code violations, which amounted to legal bribes. In other words, this guy, whom everyone knew was guilty, was living better and spending less time in jail than Kane, and Kane was relatively innocent. Clearly, this guy knew things Kane didn't. Bruno walked past Kane when the lock on the door buzzed and clicked, and Bruno paused, looked Kane in the eye, and said, "Come see me when you get out."

Kane went to see him a couple years later, and their association introduced Kane to Petey V and eventually put Kane in this room waiting for Fate's other shoe to drop.

On the small screen, the five-two Tran wore a pin-striped suit that set off his white hair, which reached the middle of his back, and wispy, white beard, which reached the middle of his chest. His round, wire-rimmed eye-glasses softened the stark lines of his face, commas for eyebrows, slanted eyes, and a hooked nose. An old friend of Kane's, a man named Tae Yoon Lee, held the door, and Tran followed a younger man into The Taproom.

"Is that Tran?" Kane asked.

Bruno said, "Looks like a midget hermit, doesn't he?"

Their eyes moved to the second screen, where Tom looked to be offering the men drinks and gesturing to the door to Pete's office.

"He doesn't look like much." Pete said.

Bruno nodded. "Don't let his size fool you. He's the only threat to us in this town."

"Is he the future?" Pete asked beneath his breath.

Kane didn't know if Tran was the future, but he knew his past because he'd read a copy of his CCPD file. Tran had been investigated for everything from murder to arson since he stepped, penniless, off a bus in 1975. Before coming to Central City, he'd been a translator for the U.S. Army in Vietnam, which meant he'd made a fortune selling black market U.S. goods to the wealthy South Vietnamese while serving the troops as a pimp and drug dealer.

He'd had to leave most of his fortune behind when he'd bribed his way onto a transport plane leaving Saigon a few months before it fell to the Vietcong, but he had friends and family on both ends of the Ho Chi Minh trail and had slowly smuggled his wealth across the Pacific in the form of military surplus, heroin, and flesh. He'd spent seventeen years in Central City consolidating his influence, first in the Vietnamese, Korean, and Hmong immigrant communities of Waite Park and eventually spreading into Uptown, The Heights, and The Hill.

Kane leaned back and closed the cabinet doors over the CCTVs before Tran and his men entered.

"Thank you for meeting me, gentlemen." Tran spoke flawless English with a slight British accent. He'd studied Engineering at the University of London in the late 'fifties. "Tae Yoon Lee works as a liaison with the Korean community, and this is my nephew Yung Van Kahn."

When Kane shook Tae's hand, Tae stared blankly at Kane's nose. They'd known one another since their time at St. Catherine's, though they had rarely seen each other during the twelve years since graduation. On opposite sides of the table, they left their past behind them.

Tran and his entourage sat. "I wanted to meet with you," Tran said, "to discuss the death of Mathew Sorenson."

"Sorenson's dead?" Pete asked.

Tran nodded. "He broke his neck slipping in the shower earlier this evening."

"You scheduled this meeting last week," Bruno said.

"Foresight never hurt anyone," Tran said. "I assure you it wouldn't have hurt Mr. Sorenson. In any event, I wanted you to know that I will be taking control of Mr. Sorenson's interests on The Hill."

"What about Jorgenson?" Bruno asked.

Tobias Jorgenson was Sorenson's brother-in-law. Everyone called him The Pastor for two reasons: He was the pastor of Bethel Lutheran Church, and he was prone to quoting scripture and generally a bit pious for a man who helped control the drug traffic, prostitution, and politics of his white-collar neighborhood. Kane had once asked him how he could reconcile his beliefs with his business interests, and he'd said, "All things are lawful unto me, but all things are not expedient."

What can you say to that?

"The Pastor?" Tran chuckled. "The Pastor will continue to tend his flock, and he will begin to pay me twenty percent for the privilege."

Everyone sat in silence for a few ticks.

Pete spoke first. "Why are you telling us?"

The most difficult conversations are the ones we never have.

"This makes us neighbors, of a sort. You control everything between Riverwalk and South Street, from St. Patrick's to the docks. I thought you'd want to know I'd be next door."

"This is a courtesy call?"

Tran ran his fingers through the length of his white

beard. "You may call it whatever you wish."

Pete said, "Tran, is there something you want to say to us?"

Tran stood and motioned for his colleagues to do the same. "I believe I've been clear enough."

When their guests were gone, Pete, Bruno, and Kane sat around the table and stared at their hands.

"That was the moment," Kane said.

Pete said, "What's that, kid?"

"That was the last best chance. We had our moment to take a stand, and it just walked out of the bar."

Bruno shook his head. "What should we have done, shot the place up?"

Pete ignored Bruno. "When did you know that?"

"I don't know."

Pete waited.

"I guess about a week ago, when Bruno told me about the meeting."

"If you knew that," Pete said, "you should've done something about it. That scar on your face makes you look tough. Too bad I know better."

"I don't get it," Bruno said. "Why did he come down here to tell us he killed Sorenson? Why was it so important for him to meet with us?"

Pete stood and held his face in his hands for a moment. When he spoke, he spoke through his fingers. "He was sizing us up. He wanted to know if we'd push back. The kid's right. He got his answer."

Bruno stood and pointed a finger at the door. "You

want him dead? We can kill that midget in the next hour. We can call a couple of guys and have his neck broken in the shower."

"Tran will go to ground," Kane said. "He'll have a small army at his house and his office in the Dragon's Mane. He won't go anywhere else for the next few weeks. If we try to hit him and fail, we'll start a war. Everyone will side with Tran because they're as afraid of us as they are of him, and we were the aggressors. He came here to show us he's not afraid, to put our backs against the wall. He came to gloat, to tell us that he killed Sorenson, but everyone will say it was an accident, even if they are suspicious. Nobody wants trouble, and he's using The Pastor as a puppet, so he's insulated."

Petey V had been watching Kane as he spoke. When he finished, Pete nodded, stood, and opened the door. "You guys get some sleep. Bruno, I'll call you tomorrow."

Bruno and Kane drove through the city in silence. Bruno dropped Kane at his Buick and waved through the side window as he drove away. When Kane reached his apartment, he heard the phone ringing as he fumbled with his keys.

No light shone beneath the door to her bedroom, and Kane hoped to silence the phone before she woke. At the start of the next ring, Kane pulled the receiver off the hook, and said, "Hello."

"Kane. It's me."

"Okay."

Kane's pager had been lighting up with calls from Detective Bayonne all night, but he hadn't had time to call the detective back.

"We need to talk. I'm a block away in The Kaiser Haus off Arapahoe."

"I'll meet you in the park."

Kane turned to leave again when her door creaked. He looked into the darkness, her diminutive, round form cloaked in shadow. She stepped forward, wearing a pink sweatshirt and pajama pants decorated with little Scottish Terriers, and smiled, the muscles in her jaw pulling the flesh upward, turning the scar tissue on her neck white. She looked so innocent, like a ten-year-old awoken from a bad dream, but the scar showed the cost she'd paid to survive forty-nine hard years.

"I need to step out for a few minutes. You going to be okay until I get back?"

She nodded.

"Try to go to sleep."

Her smile faded, and her eyes glazed over. She seemed to be looking into Kane's chest, searching for his heart. Kane walked to her and gave her a hug. Her arms hung limp at her sides.

"I'll be back as quick as I can."

***

Detective Vincent Bayonne stood beneath a lamppost on the edge of Woodland Park. He held a sack lunch in one hand and a cigarette in the other. His Army-green jacket hung loose on his thin frame, but his flannel shirt fit him well, tucked into his jeans. He watched Kane from

beneath his Detroit Pistons cap. He stuck his cigarette between his lips, an island of flesh in a sea of graying beard
that extended from his ears to his solar plexus. He held
the sack lunch toward Kane.

Kane wasn't much of a drinker, but in his line of work,
if he didn't take a sip when offered, he wouldn't be trusted.

"You know the cookhouse by Lincoln Cemetery?" Bayonne asked.

"You're here about the overdose?"

"I'm here about a murder."

Kane stood for a moment, watching the park at night,
before tugging the paper bag from the bottle's lip, taking
a pull, and passing the sack back to Bayonne. They stood
at the southeast corner of the city's largest playground,
two cracked tennis courts, a concrete slab of a basketball
court, a bathroom building adjacent to a pavilion with
four picnic tables, and the pond, beyond it all, reflect-
ing the moonlight. On the other side of the water, the
lanky figure of Herman the German towered above the
trees, lit by floodlights, a spear in one hand and a shield
in the other.

Bayonne's gaze followed Kane's. Bayonne took the cigarette from his mouth and pointed at the statue with the
two fingers gripping the nail. "Did I ever tell you who he
was and who built the statue?"

Kane smiled and nodded.

The children of the first wave of immigrants to the
city had erected the embattled Hun to defend the values
of their past from the currents of change, currents that

stemmed from their own choices and desires, but changes that appeared so foreign, so disorienting, as though they flowed against the natural order of things. Change, as always, had its way. A hundred years after the statue was built, few who lived here knew Herman's place in history, and one of the few was the French-American detective from Detroit.

"I told the fellas you'd take the case this way, Vinnie. I warned them, and I'm warning you."

"The door had been locked from the inside and closed behind the murderer. A belt had been looped around the guy's neck."

"Does it look like a struggle? When you get his blood back, you'll know for certain he was laced to the gills. He most likely overdosed."

"If he wasn't murdered, and I think he was, then he died while someone was trying to murder him."

Kane turned away from the park and motioned for Bayonne to follow him down Arapahoe toward the lake, crossing from Woodland Park into Commerce City. They walked for a while in silence. Kane thought over the situation, a situation he'd played over in his head several times since he'd first had the conversation with Bruno about Bayonne being tossed the case. Bruno had called him in the early morning, said it was a done deal, that Petey V was already making the call. Kane had said it could spin out of control. Bruno had said it already had. Bruno had said Bayonne was Kane's guy, so Kane needed to talk to him.

"If you told Pete and Bruno I'd go this way, why did they

still want me to have the case?"

"You live up by Jefferson Street. Closer to the Jefferson Precinct than St. Pat's."

Bayonne nodded.

"You used to work at Jefferson, back when you first made detective. You worked narcotics out of there. Now you drive past the Jefferson Precinct to go to work at another precinct, farther away, just to work a homicide table. I wonder why. Why does a man who grew up in Detroit and who patched up GIs in Vietnam for three years move to Central City to go out of his way to catch killers in a blue-collar paradise?"

Bayonne flicked his butt toward the street. "Maybe I've got nothing better to do. You never used to be this long-winded."

"Pete wants to know if there's something there. He wants you to have the case because he believes you are honest and meticulous but still our guy, and we're all on the same side. You'll find what needs to be found but won't make a fuss if you don't have to. I, on the other hand, didn't want you on the case because I know you. I know you won't let go of something if you don't understand it."

"Would you?"

"Yes. I've learned the hard way that sometimes you need to let things go. You can't make the world right. No one can."

Kane liked Detective Vincent Bayonne. Bayonne looked like a mountain man and a long-haul trucker had a coyote for a baby, but he had intuition. To hear him tell it, especially after a few too many drinks, murder spoke to him. All he had to do was listen. That might've been a crock of shit. Bayonne was a drunk circling the drain, but he was also the smartest cop Kane had ever met, and surprisingly honest, even with himself, even if he did believe he was a diviner of death.

"Have you ever heard the phrase live and let die?" Kane asked.

Bayonne took a pull from his bottle, passed it to Kane, and lit a second cigarette. "I was always more of a Lennon fan."

"Vladimir Ilyich Ulyanov? Listen to me, Vinnie. I'm telling you. You should let this go. Your first priority, keep this thing from blowing back on the people who keep the peace in this city. Your second priority, keep this out of the news as best you can. Third priority, close the case as soon as possible. In that order. You get me? Keep it quiet and put it to bed."

Bayonne exhaled a cloud of smoke. "You guys think highly of yourselves."

"No, we don't. We don't confuse our work with our calling, or our ideals, either."

"Your bosses are real idealists."

"Get your head right, Vinnie. You'll never be able to prove Connolly was murdered, and most people will never care. You don't just work for the city."

They were on Arapahoe near 22nd Avenue, the heart of Commerce City and a few blocks south of the old Italian neighborhood. The houses were closer together than they had been, and a tarantella emanated from the open door of a corner bar. The bartender dragged a tub of empty bottles toward the street. The rumble of their voices rippled toward the old man, a guy named Antonio who went by Antonio. Some youngster once called him Tony, and the kid had to have the glass plucked out of his cheek. Antonio looked up, saw the pair, raised a hand, paused, left the bottles on the sidewalk, and disappeared into the bar. Kane had always admired the guy, but maybe he didn't feel the same about Kane. Bayonne and Kane walked a block in silence.

After they crossed 21st Avenue, Kane turned into an alley, slid a key into a steel door, and held the door for Bayonne. Kane flipped a switch on the wall and they both squinted into the flickering fluorescence. A hardware store occupied the space on the other side of the wall, facing 20th, but the store didn't connect to the back stairs, which ascended to three floors of apartments used by girls who worked for Bruno. This early on a Wednesday, a few people might be sleeping the night off, but nobody was coming or going.

Kane opened the door to the hallway one flight up, and Bayonne waited while Kane stepped into the first apartment, which served as an office and breakroom. During business hours, a manager would take payment for the rooms and the girls, provide security, and the girls could use the space to watch television and relax between tricks. One of the bedrooms in the back had laundry machines, and the other, a locked room, had surveillance equipment connected to two of the apartments upstairs. Kane pulled a bottle off the top of the fridge and two glasses from a cupboard.

Bayonne and Kane climbed the final three flights of stairs, stopping once for Bayonne to catch his breath, and they stepped out into a clear, crisp night. The skyline glowed, and Herman stared their way, a belligerent grimace frozen above the trees. Kane poured two fingers of whiskey in each glass and set the office bottle on the ledge.

Vinnie, his sack lunch stashed in his coat, began to flick a tin between his thumb and forefinger. He jammed a wad into his lip and spit a string of fluid off the edge of the building. He took a long drink, set the lowball on the ledge, and pulled a pack of Camels out of the front pocket of his flannel.

"You aren't planning to live too long, are you, Vinnie?"

Once the nail was lit, he shook it at Kane between two fingers and exhaled between words. "I don't like this. A favor is one thing, but I told you I'd never cover up a murder."

"I'm not asking you to. I'm telling you not to make something out of nothing."

Kane watched the grizzled veteran puff and spit for a few beats. When his glass got low, Kane topped it off.

"What's this case telling you? What are you hearing as you take in the crime?"

Bayonne shook his head and looked away. "That's what bugs me. I don't hear anything. Maybe I've lost a step, but I can't hear this case."

"Doesn't that mean there isn't a case?"

"No, you don't understand. If I heard that, it would be

something. I hear nothing. Silence. There's got to be a reason for that. There's something missing, something I don't understand."

"You need to let it go. Take care of business, Vinnie, first and foremost."

They stared at the erect downtown skyline, the center of attention at the edge of the great lake. The skyscrapers dropped a few stories as the developments drifted into Midtown, whose most prominent feature was the circular shape of the Central City Chateau, the stadium. The dome of the capitol, white marble lit by multi-colored floodlights, glowed adjacent to the modern epicenter, and St. Catherine's hovered on the rise to Uptown. To their left, the neighborhoods of Kane's youth spread beyond sight, a glitter of street lamps and traffic lights, and south of the old neighborhoods spread the low-lying tenements, trailers, and broken-down homes of the south side. Could Bayonne see things from Kane's angle?

Bayonne broke the silence. "Did you know I used to live in Waite Park?"

"Did you now?"

"Before my wife died. I always hated it there, so flat and flashy. Chain stores and corporate restaurants."

"I've always loved this city, but Waite Park is the worst of it."

"Worse than SOCCs?"

"SOCCs has a lot of character, if you know how to see it. Waite Park is an aesthetic death. There's nothing there but a bunch of people waiting to die."

"You only love this city because you've never lived any-where else."

"I love this city because it's a palimpsest."

"Who do you think you're fooling with words like that?"

"The present is written on top of the past."

"Like the view of the cathedral behind the skyline or neon lights slapped on the brick facades in Commerce City."

"Exactly."

"Every midwestern city is like that."

"Why did you move here, then?"

"It seemed like the only option at the time."

"Maybe that's all Central City is, a place where peo-ple end up."

"You're still young. You could go wherever you want."

"Where else am I going to go, Vinnie? What else can I do? This is the only life available to me."

"You could finish your degree."

"I studied philosophy. Nobody's hiring philosophers."

"You could go to law school."

"Law school? I'm a felon."

"Study whatever you want, but you don't need to stay here, doing what you do."

"I'm good at what I do, and I'm not going to go around asking for a job, selling my time so someone else can make a profit. Why would I do that?"

"That's not all there is to it. Can you honestly say that you're living up to your potential? That you contribute? Don't you believe in anything?"

A few ticks passed as they stared at one another. Bayonne looked away first, and the two stared out at the city they called home, a beautiful sight if you didn't know what you were looking at.

"Look, I didn't come up here with you to talk about my mistakes or my future. Are you going to play ball or not?"

Bayonne chuckled. He took a sip of his drink and said, "Do you ever blame me for how things turned out?"

"No."

Kane felt the detective searching the side of his face, but Kane couldn't look him in the eye.

The most difficult conversations are the ones we never have.

"We searched Connolly's basement apartment this afternoon and found nothing, and we've run down most of the people who were at Mason's Monday night to Tuesday morning. Connolly got there about three-thirty. The only person who was there after three-thirty that my partner and I haven't talked to is Molly Matches, but we'll get to her. I know she's handicapped, but we need to cross her off the list at some point. The next step is to give Alfie's a once-over. Alfie's is one of Bruno's bars. I want to talk to Connolly's coworkers."

"There's only one other bartender. It's not much of an operation."

"What about Shady Pines?"

Alfie's was a shack somebody had turned into a bar twenty years ago. Bruno owned it now, and his girls worked the bar, would check out with the bartender, and take their marks across the street to a no-tell-motel called

Shady Pines.

"The Knaublachs hardly ever leave the motel, and when they do, they don't go far. I'll make sure everybody talks to you. You sure you want to go this way?"

"I'm going to do my job. If it doesn't go anywhere, I'll drop it."

THREE

OBJECTS LIKE WOMEN

10:04AM Wednesday, September 2, 1992

Alfie's was an old shed on Hill Avenue between Grant and Columbus. Technically, Alfie's was in Woodland Park, but everything south of Grant Street, from the western edge of St. Patrick's to the eastern edge of Commerce City, acted as a no-man's land providing for the less reputable commercial needs of the city's southern half.

What had once been family homes and mom-and-pop shops had been repurposed as corner bars, liquor stores, pawnshops, massage parlors, alternative clinics, C-stores, and offices for ambulance chasers, jetsam from the public defender's office, bail bondsmen, and therapists, all of which catered to the caprice of the working-class residents of the old neighborhoods and the unskilled, marginally employed, or welfare denizens of the south side.

Painted signs, shingles, and placards advertised anything and everything that distracted from the uncomfortable truth that life happened while you sought its solution for a modest fee.

The proprietors knew the fantasies and illusions of their clientele, the belief in their own self-importance, the sense of need that fueled their desires, the idea they could control their fate if they hired the proper advocate, found the proper tincture, or performed the necessary exercise, and business boomed.

Even surrounded by the sprawl of makeshift commercial fronts, Alfie's, once a machinist's shop, stood out as an eyesore. Neon beer signs lay dormant behind windows mounted in a wooden frame encased in aluminum siding. Several colors of spray paint defaced the aluminum, marking the territory with the nicknames of delinquents in rival tribes, and, on top of a pole, a faded, plastic sign declared the name Alfie's. If the cows ever came home, and don't hold your breath, they'd steer clear of this barn-turned-meat-market.

Only a few blocks north, well-kept lawns and refurbished homes framed the park and stretched north through Woodland to the river and Midtown, the nicest section of the city below Riverwalk Drive, the range to graze if seeking greener pastures.

A young woman wearing a Central City Spirits sweatshirt with matching sweatpants leaned against the front door of the bar, smoking a cigarette. Bayonne and his partner parked and stepped from the car, and she came forward and introduced herself as Sandy. In contrast to her pajamas, she'd plastered her face with makeup, thick foundation padded pink and blushed red, eyebrows drawn in, and a line of sparkling blue above each eye. Her hair, bottle-blond with an inch of brunette roots, had been pulled back and tied off. She didn't extend a hand to shake.

"Thanks for meeting us," Bayonne said, just to be polite.

"I wouldn't be here if I weren't getting paid. Let's make this quick. I've got to be back to open the place at four."

"Did Michael Connolly work Monday night?"

"We're the only two bartenders, and we're open four to two, seven days a week. Somebody better be here to take Mikey's place tonight. Last night was a shit show."

She unlocked the front door of Alfie's, held it, and stepped behind the bar and flipped a row of switches. Three walls worth of neon outshone the four naked bulbs in the ceiling, and a kaleidoscope of colors danced across the plywood walls and yellowing pine frame on which the aluminum exterior had been nailed. The collage of electricity, with an occasional metal sign slipped in, belied the benefits of ubiquitous brands of beer, liquor, cigarettes, and a variety of automobiles that appealed to needs baser and more mundane than conveyance. Speakers had been hung on the support beam, and wires stapled to the crossbeams and strung back to the stereo behind the bar. Stools sat in front of the bar, and the only other furniture consisted of folding tables and folding chairs on the concrete floor. One other room, a closet in the back, contained a toilet and plastic sink. A half-shrunk bar of soap sat on the edge of the plastic basin. Bayonne had seldom seen a sadder excuse for a bar.

Bayonne's voice echoed in the cavernous space. "What does it sound like when it rains?"

"We crank the music."

"Does it get cold in the winter?"

"We've got space heaters, but no matter how cold it gets outside, when we're packed, it's downright hot."

"Who are your customers?" Adam asked.

Both Sandy and Bayonne turned to look at Adam.

"What do you mean?" she asked.

"How would you describe your clientele? Who comes here?"

"They're not my clientele." She spit out the last word. "We get people who like to drink. A lot. Isn't that obvious?"

Bayonne stared at his partner for a few beats before gesturing for him to take the floor. "Do you have any other questions?"

Adam shook his head and folded his arms across his belly. When he got nervous, Bayonne had noticed, Adam absentmindedly tried to hide his girth.

Bayonne took the tin from his back pocket, flicked it between his thumb and forefinger, and turned to Sandy. "Did anything out of the ordinary happen on Monday night?"

"Out of the ordinary?"

"Were there any fights? Did anybody threaten Mr. Connolly? Anything like that?"

"People threatened Mikey every night he worked. He broke up three or four fights that night, and we were a little slow."

Bayonne shoved a wad into his mouth. He figured he was wasting his time, just trying to chase a feeling. If Sandy knew something, she wouldn't tell the police about it. Connolly's apartment had been a bust, and they had statements from almost everyone who'd been at Mason's and gotten nothing. There wasn't another move, not that Bayonne could see. He turned in a circle, his eyes taking in the urban blight around him. He'd thought something would jump out. If he followed the links in the case, he thought he'd start to hear it, and sooner or later, he'd understand. He didn't hear shit, so he tried to think of questions to ask, questions that weren't stupid.

"You two are real jokers, aren't you?" Sandy commented. "Face it. Mikey overdosed. He was a fun guy, but he smoked or spiked anything he could get his hands on. He was bound to end this way."

Beneath her three feet of makeup and the social anxieties that makeup attempted to hide, this angel had some balls, and she was shaking them in Bayonne's face. She knew he and Adam were chasing their tails, hoping to catch something worth clinging to. The woman's eyes, their dullness hidden behind fifty shades of mascara, stared at Bayonne's impotence with what he took to be a mixture of sorrow and rage.

She looked away and her voice softened. "I wish there was someone you could blame for Mike, but there isn't. Mike is the only person to blame. You should leave it alone."

Bayonne had been hearing that a lot lately.

"The girls who work the bar take their guys across the street to Shady Pines?" Bayonne asked.

"Yeah. They check out with us at the bar and pay Ben or Brian over there. That way the girl doesn't need to carry money around, and she can get it whenever she wants, twenty-four hours a day."

"Who was working Shady Pines Monday night?"

"Brian's the night manager, and Ben works the office during the day. They're brothers, and they're simple. Not quite kids but not quite adults."

"The working girls trust them to hold their money?"

"We all work for the same people. If there was ever a problem, it would be taken care of. The girls wouldn't lose a dime no matter what. Nobody's going to rob this place, and Ben and Brian would never try anything. They don't think like that. Besides, where else are they going to work? This is a dream job for them."

"Ben is over there now?"

"They both are. They live there and only ever leave to go to the store. They're the kind of guys who are forty years old and still watch cartoons and play with fireworks."

The Shady Pines Motor Inn was an L-shaped monstrosity that had been painted pink twenty years ago and never touched up. A front office faced Hill Avenue, a small room with a desk, folding chair, and a television behind a bullet-proof plastic window with a little tray that slides beneath, so people can pay. Fourteen rooms draped around the parking lot. Plastic patio furniture circled a concrete ash tray in front of every third room. The plastic sign on the edge of the street said: Nightly/Hourly/Weekly/Monthly above the word __cancies. Cancies must be one of the diseases you could get if you slept there.

Bayonne, Adam, and Sandy crossed the street to the office to speak with Ben, who talked out of one side of his mouth as though he'd had a stroke or two. He examined Bayonne's badge through the translucent barrier for what seemed like an eternity before waddling over to use the phone. He spoke into the handset for a few minutes, set the handset on his desk, waddled back to Bayonne, and yelled through the holes drilled at the bottom of his cage, "Are you Detective Bi-un?"

Bayonne looked at Sandy, and she said, "You two should get along."

Bayonne held his badge and ID up to the plastic again.

Ben stared at it, put a finger in his nose, and leaned down to the communication vent. "Are you Detective Bi-un?"

"Yes, I am."

He waddled back to the phone and spoke into the headset again before hanging up, taking a set of keys off a hook, and stepping out of his cage. He smiled at Bayonne, and said, "We better go wake up Brian."

Ben led the way across the parking lot. A woman in a pink bathrobe, her hair in curlers, cradled a terrier mix in her left hand, smoked a cigarette with her right, and watched the procession through pink sunglasses. Bayonne nodded to her, and she smiled.

Ben stopped in front of the door farthest from the office

and knocked. He waited a few moments, knocked again, chose a key from the wad dangling off his belt, unlocked the door, and stepped into the room. A soap opera played out on a television surrounded by pizza boxes, Doritos bags, and empty Pepsi two-liters. When Ben turned on the light, his half-naked mirror image sat up in the nearest of the two double beds.

Brian farted and wiped his eyes.

"The police are here, and you're supposed to answer their questions. Boss says." Ben stepped around Bayonne and paused in the doorway, and his voice rose in pitch but not volume. "And clean this place up. Do you think you live in a barn or something? Jeez."

Brian scratched his armpit. "I'm sorry for my brother. He's not too bright."

Ben shook his head as he waddled back across the parking lot.

Brian and Ben may have been twins. They both stood about six-foot-four, and their bulging bellies suggested they were either pregnant or that their sedentary lives had gotten the better of them. They both exhibited early signs of the late stages of male pattern baldness, and they both spoke out of the sides of their mouths, though opposing sides.

Once Brian had put on sweatpants and a t-shirt decorated with a clutch of Care Bears driving a cloud car, Bayonne asked him about Sunday night. He shrugged, yawned, and said things were pretty quiet.

"Did anything out of the ordinary happen?"

Brian cleared his throat a few times and stared at the television for a minute before turning back to Bayonne. "One of the girls never picked up her money. Is that ordinary?"

"Had it happened before?"

"No."

"Sounds out of the ordinary. You're saying a prostitute didn't pick up her money?"

"We're not supposed to use that word."

"What word would you use?"

"I don't know. I usually just use their names."

"What was this girl's name?"

"I don't know."

"Why don't you tell me what happened?"

"A guy paid. I took his money and gave him a key. The girls are supposed to come in, too, but not this time. He didn't know the girl's name, so I put her money in an envelope in the cash box and wrote nerd, the time, and room number on it."

Brian stepped into the bathroom but left the door open, and Bayonne heard the sound of water hitting porcelain.

"Nerd?"

"Yeah. The guy came around a lot. Most weekends. He seemed like a nerd."

Bayonne turned to Sandy. "Do you know who he's talking about?"

"I don't know. Monday night? Thick glasses and a silk shirt?"

"That sounds like him." Brian walked past Bayonne and

Sandy and stood next to Adam on the concrete in front of his room. The big man stretched, exposing the holes in his armpits. He pointed at Adam. "He looked like him only skinny and taller."

"Art Spencer," Sandy said.

"Did you see the prostitute?" Bayonne asked.

Sandy said, "The only girls working that night were Diamond and Cindy. They both left around midnight when the party turned the corner."

Brian smiled. "They're always nice to me. They both stopped by to talk. Sometimes Cindy brings me candy."

Bayonne said, "Neither of them claimed the money?"

"They'd already left when the guy came over. I told Mike about it, and he said he didn't know. The girls are supposed to check out with Mike or Sandy and then check in with us. We're supposed to keep them safe."

Bayonne watched the big man, soft as a teddy bear. How would he keep somebody safe?

"Was Mike angry about the girl not checking out with him?"

"We'd been paid. He took the bar's cut. Mike didn't care as long as we were paid."

Bayonne nodded.

"He'd been pretty drunk, still in room four when Ben took over. I mentioned it to him, told him we'd need to charge the guy for the whole day."

"The john didn't check out with you?"

"He hadn't checked out when I got off this morning. I don't know if he checked out with Ben. We haven't needed the room yet."

"You mean he's still there? He's been there since yesterday morning?"

"I don't know. Maybe. He's a regular. If he doesn't pay when he leaves, he'll pay next time."

"How often does he stay the night?"

"He's never done that before, but it can happen. Sometimes people stay for days if they're sick, and they leave a mess. The nerd usually just pays for an hour."

Bayonne pointed down the row of rooms. "You said room four?"

"Room four is the fourth one from the office."

Made sense.

Sandy, Adam, and Bayonne crossed the parking lot.

"Do you think we're on to something?" Adam asked.

"I don't know. I don't know what to think."

Sandy pointed to a 1986 Ford Escort station wagon parked on Hill Avenue on the other side of the motel's office. "That's Art Spencer's car."

The woman in the bathrobe lit another cigarette, exhaled a cloud of smoke, and watched through the shade of her rose-colored glasses.

**

Ben had never spoken to the man in room four. He'd never seen the man until he opened the door and saw him in his all-together, hands folded as if in prayer, with a belt wrapped around his neck.

"My god, is that what Mikey looked like?" Sandy asked.

Bayonne shrugged. "That's how he was posed."

Sandy spun on her heel and walked toward Hill Avenue and Alfie's across the street. Bayonne called out to her, and she quickened her pace.

Bayonne told Ben to wait in his office and turned to Adam, who was sitting on the concrete with his head between his knees and his eyes squeezed shut. "You okay?"

"I'll be fine in a minute."

"How are you going to be a detective if you can't handle dead bodies?"

"It's not that." Adam stood, took a deep breath and two steps into the parking lot. "It's not the body. It's the way it's posed. It reminds me of something. I get a flash, a bunch of sound, like a memory that I can't quite picture, and I feel sick. I'm sorry."

"Don't apologize to me. Just pull yourself together and go radio this in. We need a patrol car, a medical examiner, and a forensic unit out here to run the scene."

As Adam stumbled toward the Vega, Bayonne spit the wad in his lip into the parking lot and turned back to room four. He took a soft pack out of his shirt pocket, shook a cigarette into his hand, put it in his mouth, lit it, and rubbed his forehead while he breathed smoke into his lungs. His eyes drifted across every detail, major or minor.

The room contained one double bed, the comforter stained and torn, a folding chair in the corner, and plastic vertical blinds. Cigarette burns pockmarked the carpet, and mold was visible on the back of the window air conditioner, a water spot on the carpet beneath.

The man was sprawled on the top of the bed, on top

of the comforter, which probably wasn't too comforting, and he still wore thick, horn-rimmed glasses. He had a bad case of back acne and a hairy ass. His eyes bulged as though he'd gained consciousness just in time for one last gasp.

Bayonne placed his smoke on the edge of the window sill and stepped into the room. Without touching the body, he gave it a closer once over and couldn't see any signs of violence. The man's clothes had been folded in a neat pile on a chair near the bed, and Bayonne found the guy's wallet and confirmed he had once been Art Spencer. He found a ring of keys with a Ford emblem on one, a pack of Juicy Fruit, and two unused condoms. Other than a well-worn Gideon's Bible, the rest of the room was empty.

Bayonne took a long swig from his flask, figured he'd seen everything there was to see, and stepped back onto the walkway in front of the rooms. He put the cigarette from the window sill back in his mouth and closed his eyes, doing his best to listen.

Nothing. Nothing but a sour stench of decaying flesh.

The corpse, having sat in the room more than twenty-four hours, had begun to smell.

Why couldn't he hear anything? At least he had a case now, but Bayonne had never had a case this stubborn. He looked for an answer in the parking lot, and the woman in the bathrobe sitting with her terrier in front of a door on the far wing smiled, cocked her head, raised her sunglasses, and winked.

Bayonne walked over, sat down next to her, and offered her a cigarette.

The woman's terrier hopped off her lap and growled at the grizzled detective.

"Spike, go to bed." The woman slid a Virginia Slim from a hard pack and placed it between her lips, and Spike disappeared into room nine.

Bayonne took the zippo out of his pocket and offered to light her smoke, but she leaned away and used a miniature Bic.

"You call your terrier Spike?"

"That's her name." She spoke while holding the Virginia Slim with her teeth. "You sure are pushy for a man who's been ignoring me all morning."

"I wasn't ignoring you. I just didn't want to disturb you. That's all."

"I could've saved you time. You didn't need to talk to all these hoopleheads just to find that body. I knew it was in there."

"What's your name, miss?"

"You've walked by me three times now. I tried to help, but you didn't want to give me the time of day. Now you want to know my name?"

"I'm sorry about that. We should've stopped by and paid you the proper respect first thing."

"That's right. You should've, but you didn't. I hope you're learning a thing or two."

Bayonne used the butt of his smoke to light a fresh one and stamped the butt into the ash tray before leaning back in his chair and taking his flask from his coat. He considered what she'd said and took a nip.

She patted his arm. "Don't feel bad. You haven't lost a step. I just don't think this case is about you."

Bayonne looked her full in the face for the first time and realized he couldn't see her features behind her sunglasses.

"It's written all over your face," she said. "Besides, I watched you stand over there and try to listen, like you were going to figure things out without working at it."

Bayonne chuckled. He hadn't thought about it that way.

"Kids these days," she said.

"I'm not exactly a kid."

"These things are relative. Anyway, if you fly like a duck, you get shot at like a duck."

"What's that supposed to mean?"

"You need to ask the right questions and look this thing in the face. You need to roll up your sleeves on this one."

"What questions should I ask?"

"Try this one on for size. Did the bartender know?"

"Sandy?"

"Who's that?"

"The woman who was with us."

"Not her, the other bartender. The man."

"Michael Connolly?"

"Whatever his name is. He didn't give me the time of day, either, but he knew about the body in there. I can tell you that much."

"Connolly knew?"

"He most certainly did."

"How do you know that?"

"He stopped in after his shift at two forty-seven yesterday morning. He wanted to get the money for the room. I think he'd been drinking."

"Two forty-seven? That's pretty precise."

She tugged on the sleeve of her bathrobe and showed Bayonne her Timex.

"What did he do? Was he with Brian or Ben?"

"He got the key from Brian, walked in, and turned the light on so I could see the body on the bed from out here. He was in there for a while, like he was looking for something. Then he turned the light out, locked the door, and was muttering something about how he wouldn't clean up the mess this time." She leaned toward Bayonne, and he doubted she'd brushed her teeth in a while. "Like I said, I think he'd been drinking."

Bayonne pulled on his flask. "You didn't happen to see the dead guy go into the room with anyone, did you?"

"It's not like I sit here all the time. I watch my shows too, you know. He must've gone in there before midnight. I was watching reruns of 'Mary Tyler Moore' on Nick at Nite." She dragged on her Virginia Slim and took a sip from an opaque plastic cup. "You know things didn't used to be like this."

Bayonne sat back and flicked ash onto the blacktop.

"When I was a kid," she said, "Hill Avenue was a dirt road. There were only four houses on it south of Grant, all country homes. Only the O'Malley place is still standing."

Bayonne figured the old broad to be knocking on eighty; she might've been a bit younger but weathered from some of her habits.

"People used to treat people all right back then." She took a long drink. "People were decent."

"Things aren't the way they used to be." Bayonne neglected to add that they never were. He'd never begrudge someone the lies their memories told them. He appreciated a good false memory now and again, especially when the days blended into the nights.

"Oh, how would you know." She sipped from her cup, rolled the liquid around on her tongue, and swallowed. "You think I'm kidding myself. Well, maybe I am. I suppose people were always scoundrels."

"It's unnerving when you do that."

"Then keep your thoughts to yourself."

Adam appeared at Bayonne's side. "What are you two talking about?"

"You wouldn't understand, young man." The old woman stamped out her Virginia Slim and pushed herself out of her chair. Adam reached forward to help her, and she slapped his hands away. "I'm not some shameless hussy you can play grab ass with. Besides, you're not my type."

Bayonne said, "What is your type?"

"Tall, dark, handsome, and rich. Good luck with your case, boys. A couple of kiddos like you two should crack this old chestnut in no time. Not that anybody cares what I think, but maybe you should get off your asses and do some actual police work. I've got my shows to watch."

The old broad disappeared into room number nine, and Bayonne waved to the medical examiner who wheeled a gurney in front of room four while two patrolmen put up tape.

"Help the patrolmen secure the scene and then help them canvas the motel to see if anybody saw anything."

Adam nodded but didn't say he was happy about being back on patrol his second day as a detective.

Bayonne walked across the street and found Sandy inside Alfie's, pouring herself a shot of vodka and wiping away her tears.

"If you're pouring, I'll take a whiskey."

Sandy set him up. "You said that's how you found Mikey?"

Bayonne nodded.

"I heard there'd been others," she said. "Everyone has been talking about this on the street. I just didn't think it was real."

"What others?"

"The other johns. My god, the person who is killing johns killed Mike."

"Back up. What other johns?"

"Mike wasn't the first."

She told Bayonne about them. They'd found a john posed like that in Shady Pines three weeks ago, and Michael Connolly had dumped the body. Mike thought it was an overdose, so they didn't want the police involved. A week and a half ago, rumors started floating around about another john dying the same way, posed the same way. Nobody knew exactly where, and nobody Sandy knew had actually seen it. She'd heard that body had been dumped too, and people thought there might be some bad smack around.

"The girls joked about the overdoses the way people do when they're trying to hide their fear. Everybody's afraid of a bad dose. Nobody really thought it was murder. It was supposed to just be a joke."

"What do you know about Art Spencer?"

"I think he might've been an accountant or something. He always added up his bill in his head and wanted to correct me for overcharging or undercharging him for drinks, even when he was hammered. Who cares if they're undercharged? He was a weird guy.

"On Monday night, he arrived late, and he'd already been drinking. He came around most weekends, and he usually did that, only came around after he was toasted, like he had to get loose before he could commit to slumming."

"Is it that much of a commitment?"

"For some, I guess so." She stared at the concrete floor.

"He had a buddy," she said, "some real estate guy from Uptown. They liked to come south of the river together."

"What was this buddy like?"

"He was an asshole. Art was an awkward dude, but his buddy was a snake, in it for himself. Bart or Bert or something. I never really talked to him, tried not to, anyway. He and Mikey were friends, though."

Bayonne wrote down what she'd said and walked back to Shady Pines. Forensics had arrived and stood waiting for the ME to remove the body. Bayonne pulled Adam aside.

"We've got something. There may have been two murders before Spencer and Connolly, and the bodies were dumped by people who assumed they were overdoses."

"Who would do that?"

"Anybody who didn't want to draw attention to their business. Michael Connolly for one. We'll check at the morgue to see if we can identify the victims."

Bayonne's heart beat faster, and his mind quickened. He was in it now. They had a case.

FOUR

MATCHES AND SPARKS

3:26PM Wednesday, September 2, 1992

Kane parallel-parked his four-door Buick Regal in front
of Seth's apartment and killed the engine without shut-
ting off the battery, taking a minute to get into character, clarify his objectives, and finish listening to "If You
Have to Ask."

As the rhythmic guitar licks wound down, his mind
rolled, stretched, and turned to land on the first time he'd
heard the song. Seth had played *Blood, Sugar* at The Saddle,
and Kane had sat transfixed as a young woman contorted
on stage. It had been the middle of the day, and only two
or three patrons watched the dancer, her eyes closed while
she mouthed the lyrics along with Anthony Kiedis. She
appeared to enjoy her own sexuality more than anyone
else in the room. When the song ended, she'd groped on

hands and knees for her clothes and the few dollars that had fluttered to the stage. Without a stitch of modesty, she stood and strutted toward the dressing room. Her tight ass and pert breasts fell flat with Kane, but he admired the insulation she'd erected, barriers stronger and more impenetrable than any chastity belt, barriers built of ignorance, aversion, and solitude.

Kane knew her and knew what she would look like in a few years, after the attitude cracked and eroded from the relentless waves of experience.

If you have to ask?

The dancer knew what she knew now because she'd never learned to ask certain difficult questions. What she wouldn't know in a few years would determine the path her life would take.

Kane liked the song but knew the song's premise was horseshit. There's no magical "it" to get. The more you ask, the more you learn, and, ultimately, the most inquisitive and open minds learn the most. But there isn't a whole lot of power or influence in that approach. The more you know, the less you know you can control.

Where's the fun in that?

The dancer expected men to respond to her in a certain way because they always had, but she never wondered why. She never questioned the depth of their feelings or their honesty, or their motivations, or her own, not, at least, as they related to her sway over them. She went with what felt familiar, as we all often do, especially when our perspective is framed by the shortsightedness of youth or the egocentricity of greed.

For better or worse, Kane had turned away from the stage and questioned his intuitions, questioned his vantage point, and pushed himself to ask questions beyond his answers.

Kane hadn't answered all his questions, but he had learned a few things about his objectives. "If You Have to Ask" helped him get into character, to shift back into the two-dimensionality his role often required, a two-dimensionality that allowed for control and influence.

Sitting in his Buick in front of Seth's apartment that late afternoon in September, Kane felt the life drain out of his eyes and a coldness creep up his spine. He pulled his keys, stepped to the curb, and walked through the dying grass to ascend the front steps.

Seth lived on the ground floor of a three-story house that had been redesigned for three apartments, one on each floor. The storm door opened to a small entryway, a converted porch containing Seth's door and a stairwell ascending to the other two apartments. Kane knocked on his door, but nobody answered, so Kane let himself in. The door was unlocked.

Molly sat on the couch, staring out the side window at parked cars and trees. She wore her platinum hair cropped short and molded around her face like an old-fashioned cartoon character, painted with a single stroke of a thick brush. Her gray eyes, once a deep blue, had faded with time and distance, but her skin, despite years of abuse, remained unblemished, smooth as the driven snow.

The muted television on cinder blocks a few feet in front of her showed a new episode of Seinfeld. A card table, a weight bench, an inclined plane, and a punching bag were the only other pieces of furniture. Blue jeans, sweat pants, basketball shorts, sweatshirts, boxers, a-shirts, and t-shirts lay where they'd fallen across the floor and workout equipment, as though someone disrobed daily to pump iron vigorously and naked.

Kane sat down next to Molly Matches.

"How you doing? Did you have a good day off?"

She turned to Kane and smiled. She wore a collared polo completely buttoned, a man's shirt, but the collar hid the scar on her neck.

"I need to ask you something, okay? And I need you to be honest. You might need to write down your answers."

Her eyes looked past Kane, to the television set, so Kane reached into her purse and took out the notepad and pen she always kept with her. He set them in her lap.

"Were you at Jimmy Mason's the night before last?"

She turned her gaze to meet his and nodded, quickly, almost imperceptibly, once.

"Did anything happen while you were there? Did you see anything that was off or weird, anything suspicious?"

She stared at him for a while as though she were studying his face, memorizing him. She shrugged.

"What were you doing there? You don't need to go to places like that, not anymore."

She picked up the pen and scribbled. He glanced at the television. Jerry was in bed with a gorgeous woman, way out of his league, and he looked to be explaining why things weren't working out.

Something happen? Like what?

Kane read her note twice and studied the side of her face as she stared out the window. The blankness of her face hid any depths of feeling. Her expressions, when she made a face, which was seldom, always seemed forced, like she was adopting an appearance she felt expected. Most of the time, she kept to herself, gazing off somewhere, remaining at the periphery of the group or situation, yet she was always around, almost as though she was always observing but never participating.

"Did anyone get hurt?"

People hurt. It happens. Why ask me? She met Kane's gaze.

"If anything happened while you were there, I want you to keep it to yourself. You should tell me, but don't tell anyone else. Okay?"

Nothing to tell.

"Something's going on, and I want you to be safe."

She smiled and nodded.

"I want you to stay away from places like that, at least for a little while. They might be dangerous right now, and I don't want anything to happen to you."

She nodded, but didn't smile.

Kane gave her a smile and squeezed her shoulder. "You can trust me. I want to help you."

Seth emerged from the bedroom wearing sweatpants and no shirt. He pulled a coffee filter from his cupboard and started to scoop Folgers out of a can. At six feet six inches, he looked like he had workout equipment for furniture.

"How are things?" he asked. "Business as usual?"

"Everything's fine. Thanks for watching Molly. Bayonne was at Alfie's and Shady Pines today."

"What brought him there?"

"He's looking into Mike Connolly's death."

"Why is he looking into an overdose?"

"Bayonne thinks there's more to it."

"You thought he might."

"He's a hell of a detective."

Amber, a twenty-two-year-old who worked at The Saddle, also wearing sweatpants and no shirt, emerged from the bedroom. She didn't look like she had exercise equipment for furniture, but she didn't look like she needed it, either.

"Hey, Kane. What are you doing here?"

Amber, like everyone at The Side Saddle other than Seth and Karla, didn't realize Kane owned the bar. She thought Kane was a go-between, middle management, for Bruno and Petey V, the guys who owned all or part of many of the bars in Woodland Park, Central City, and parts of St. Patrick's. The idea wasn't much of a stretch. Kane did work for those guys and spent most of his time bartending at Bruno's, but he owned The Saddle, two other bars, a bowling alley, car wash, and three rental properties. After hours, Kane owed those guys nothing more than monthly protection.

Amber took a mug out of the cupboard and leaned

against the counter, waiting for the coffee to drip. She scratched an itch beneath the silicone on the left side of her chest.

"Amber, honey," Seth said. "Why don't you swing by Starbucks on your way home?"

"You know where I live. Where am I going to find a Starbucks?"

Seth didn't respond, and when Amber realized he wasn't going to, she snorted in disgust, slammed the coffee cup on the counter, and stormed into the bedroom. A few moments later she emerged in a skintight leopard-skin one-piece and bounced the front door off the sheetrock.

Seth rolled his eyes.

"Is that what you call watching Molly?"

"Molly is happy. Amber, she stopped by in the afternoon. Unexpected. She was bored. I gave her entertainment."

Seth's speech pattern had been shaped by his Polish childhood. His mother, to this day, spoke English poorly and only when necessary. His father had run a club in Warsaw that catered to the Russians. When the Cold War thawed, and tides began to shift in the 'seventies, the father saw the writing on the iron curtain, decided to pull up stakes, and brought his wealth and predilections to The States. Unfortunately, Seth's father underestimated some of the people in Central City, and he was killed a couple of years after they arrived, when Seth was a teenager. Seth wound up at St. Catherine's, where he and Kane became friends. They'd been friends ever since. Seth was one of the few people Kane trusted, at least to a point.

"I saw Tae Yoon Lee the other day," Kane said.

"Tae? I heard he works for Tran now."

"He does. Tran referred to him as a liaison for the Korean community."

"A liaison. That is one word for it. Why was Tran explaining Tae's role to you?"

"There's a lot going on right now. We need to be sharp."

"I am always sharp."

"Your house is a mess, and you neglect the handicapped to bang a whore in the middle of the afternoon."

"Molly has the cleaning job. She works for me. I am not her babysitter. She has the television. I am not a monk, like you, who wants to control every little thing, manipulating from the shadows. I live this life for the money and the women. You should let your hair down, too. It would be good for your blood pressure."

Kane considered pushing him a little harder but didn't want to overdo it. Good at his job because he was a simple man with simple tastes, Seth would never try too hard because he had no desire to be his own boss. He'd seen how that had worked out for his father. When they were both kids, they'd become friends because their approaches to life meshed well despite being polar opposites. Seth, though as flawed as the next man, was honest in his way.

Kane had only wanted to get his attention, so he raised his hands in apology, backing off his high horse.

"You've got a point, but hear me when I say this, old friend. There's more going on right now than you realize. We need to tighten things up. You need to know what's going on with the girls at The Saddle, where they party and who they work for in their off hours, and we need to get the cops to look somewhere else for their killer, if there even is one. Those are our priorities right now. When I ask you to do something, even a small favor. I need you to do it, or I'll stop asking."

Molly watched the two men from the sofa.

"You do not think Bayonne will find Connolly's death an overdose?"

"I'm saying there's no Starbucks near my house, either."

Seth nodded, filled Kane's cup with coffee, and filled his own. He glanced at Molly, smiled, and motioned for Kane to follow him outside. On the porch, he pulled a soft pack of Winstons out of the pocket of his sweatpants and set his coffee cup on the railing while he lit the nail. "Will Bayonne connect Mikey to the other two overdoses?"

"It's only a matter of time. When Bayonne sees the reports, he'll make the connection."

"I did not know this would become an issue. Had I known the body should not be found, I would have put it in the lake."

"Don't worry about it. You thought it was an overdose. We all did."

"There is something else. Amber asked me for a favor, and I said I would talk to you about a girl who came into The Saddle the other day."

"Is this my way of paying for your good time?"

"Perhaps. These things have a way of balancing out, I think. This girl said she was eighteen, but I do not think she was older than seventeen, maybe sixteen. The ID she gave me was from New Mexico. No reflective surface. She did not know the capitol of New Mexico when I asked her."

"You don't know the capitol of New Mexico."

"She did not know that, either. Her sister is a girl named Diamond, a junkie, worse than any of the other girls. Amber says the mom is the same way."

Kane took a sip of his coffee and thought over the possibilities. Where had this streak of compassion come from? Below the waist, probably.

"What do you know about the mom?"

"Only what Amber says. She and Diamond were friends before Di got so bad that she is hard to be around. Di did not even care her sister wanted the job. It was like she did not notice or did not comprehend."

A few ticks passed. Kane tried not to feel the guilt that hung between them, unspoken.

"Karla wanted to turn the girl out. She said of the girl, her age made her more valuable. I sent the kid away, but now I am worried. Amber said she might be on the streets. The girl said she needed money. I gave her a twenty, told her Di could pay me back. The girl did not even smile. Could you find her, maybe give her a job or something?"

"Charity?"

"You are a good guy, Kane. Everyone knows that. You help people when you can."

"Nobody knows what everybody knows."

"The kid lives in The Corner. I have the address in my room. She looks like Diamond only younger, less tan, and less strung out. Amber said she saw her on Cheyenne. Will you try to find her?"

"I'll see what I can do tomorrow."

"Thanks, buddy. I will put the address on the counter, and I am going to shower. I want to get to The Saddle."

Kane felt the pager on his belt vibrate. He unclipped the black square and glanced at the number scrolling across the top: Detective Bayonne's office number.

"Mind if I use your phone? I believe Bayonne made the connection."

"Use the one in the bedroom. It is more private."

When Kane heard the water running in the shower, he dialed the number.

Bayonne picked up before the second ring. "Detective Bayonne."

"Vinnie, it's me."

"It turns out Michael Connolly wasn't the first victim. I've got a report on my desk of a John Doe found in a dumpster that had been posed in a similar way. Cause of death, asphyxiation. I've got another body in the morgue downtown that was found in a back alley. Cause of death an overdose of opiates and tranquilizers. Ligature marks on the neck that look like they came from a belt. The autopsy shows that it may have been posed, too, but the wrists and arms had been broken to disguise it. What's going on here?"

"Why are you asking me?"

"You knew. You knew the whole time that Connolly wasn't the first. That's why Pete wanted me to have the case."

"We all take a dim view of murder, Vinnie."

"Do we? Because it sounds like some of us are trying to cover it up."

"Everybody thought those two were overdoses. Dumping the bodies is good business, better than drawing attention to our clubs. The second one seemed a little weird, sure. The bodies were posed the same way, but nobody knew that at the time. They were discovered by different people who did their best to take care of the situation. By the time word got to somebody who could put two and two together, it was too late."

"We found the body of a guy named Art Spencer in Shady Pines this morning. He was posed the same way and had also been choked out while high."

Damn.

"What do you want me to say, Vinnie. It sounds like you've got your hands full."

"I want you to tell me if you're hiding anything else. Save me some time here. What else am I going to come across that you knew about already?"

"I didn't know the two overdoses were connected, and I didn't know about them getting dumped until after the fact, once Connolly's body was found. That's when Pete called me about giving you the case."

A few ticks passed.

"You didn't want to tell me this the other night?"

"I want this thing wrapped up as soon as possible, before it fucks up my action."

"Four people are dead. This isn't about your action. Not

anymore. There's nothing else you want to tell me?"

"I don't know anything else."

"Have it your way. I'll be in touch."

Bayonne hung up the phone, and Kane stared at his handset for a few seconds before placing it on the receiver. Bayonne had the scent now, and there'd be no stopping him.

Kane stepped out of the bedroom and saw Molly watching television. At least he could do his best to keep her safe. He sat down next to her. She watched him out of the corner of her eyes.

"You need to be smart, take care of yourself. Don't go to any more of those parties. Do you understand me? You have a home, people who care about you. Why not enjoy it?"

She scribbled and handed him the pad. *I enjoy.* Her smile reached no higher than her nose.

"Don't you like living with me?"

She nodded.

"You don't need to work at The Saddle. You could stay home or get a tutor, someone who will teach you sign language. I could learn, too. We could talk more."

Nothing to say.

"You can do whatever you want, live however you want."

What you want?

"I want you to be happy."

I'm this.

That made sense to Kane at the time. Nobody can fight who or what she is, and Kane couldn't push Molly any harder. Maybe he should've done things differently, but he didn't know how. Kane told her he loved her and gave her a hug. He could hear lips moving in his ear, her silent mouth trying to speak. He didn't think she was crying. When he looked at her face, it was dry.

FIVE

A PAVED PARADISE

9:58AM Thursday, September 3, 1992

"I don't know what happened," Bayonne said. "I don't know who the killer is or why they did what they did. Between us, though, and just between us, these murders have been covered up by people who thought the guy died during a bit of rough trade and the girl split, or the guy got a bit of bad smack. Either way, that sort of thing happens down here. They didn't want the hassle. As it turns out, you add all the guys together and the deaths were something else. The bodies had to come to light, so they toss us Michael Connolly. We've gotta solve this thing without things looking corrupt, without chasing down some bullshit charges we couldn't stick, and without the force looking incompetent."

Bayonne and Adam had taken Hill Avenue straight north through The Hill, a middle-class neighborhood where fathers mowed their own lawns and kids played in front yards on the weekend. Each house was distinct, wood panel siding left over from the early 'eighties or older, brick homes that dated back to the 'fifties, even a few nineteenth century homes on larger lots. Hill Avenue rose gently after it crossed the river, and when they crested the hill which gave the street and the neighborhood their names, they could see the steeple of First Lutheran poking through the trees on the western slope and the capitol framed by the skyline on their right. The view took Bayonne's breath away, as it always did, for that three-block stretch where he could see to the lakeshore.

"When I was on patrol, I knew things were corrupt," Adam said. "I knew the wheels were greased a little so that things could get done. I took a hat now and again."

He referred to taking a twenty or so, the price of a hat, for some information or to handle a situation a certain way when word came down to do so. He might not have even done anything. In the right precinct, on the right patrol, the hat made sure everybody felt good about everything, everybody on the same side.

"I know how things are," Adam continued. "We're not going to stop people from having their fun. I just didn't think things would be like this. Not on homicide. This is, what, four murders? For Christ's sake . . .."

"We were handed a shit show, no question." Bayonne squinted into the pockmarked glare of his windshield made translucent by the rising sun. "Things weren't always this way. They used to be a lot worse."

"What are you talking about? Worse how?"

"When I joined the force back in 'seventy-one, we still fought the good fight. By the late 'seventies, Tran Van Kahn began to consolidate Waite Park, and the wops in Commerce City were at the mick's throats in St. Patrick's. It got so you couldn't walk across the street without camouflage. There'd be a shooting in a Safeway parking lot in the middle of the afternoon, and nobody would talk to the cops. If a fight broke out in a bar, everybody was in the bathroom. We couldn't do a thing but put up tape and put bodies on ice."

They drove a couple blocks in silence. Bayonne said, "Civilians got caught in the crossfire. I canvassed a neighborhood in Waite Park after a school bus took a left into a gunfight. The driver was following his route and hadn't heard the shots over the shouting kids and diesel engine. The bus looked like swiss cheese."

Adam opened his mouth but couldn't phrase the question.

"Nobody died," Bayonne said, "but an eight-year-old and a twelve-year-old had to go through a lot of rehab. Their lives were never the same. And nobody saw a thing, not even the driver."

"How is that possible?"

"People were scared. You can't blame them. Some of those guys were real bastards and might've hurt those kids worse if somebody had talked."

"So, what happened? How did things change?"

"One of the politicians who'd been backed by either

Petey V or Elmore Washington approached the detectives on the case. Next thing you know, some witnesses show up and give precise statements about who shot up the bus. They were even willing to testify. Arrests were made, and witnesses came forward for a few other open cases."

"Was this on the level?"

"A lot of it was, and in exchange other cases were closed without arrests. We started raiding DiVittorio and Washington's competition, and they backed Tran, the lead horse in Waite Park. They were tired of fighting and losing money."

"That's how the police were bought?"

"We kept the peace. Within two months, the violence was over and there's been peace ever since. Everyone stayed in their neighborhood, got along fine, and kids could walk to school."

"And if the right person committed a murder, we'd look the other way."

"Call it what you want. We were given this case because they thought I could handle it, and, probably, to get you on board or cut you loose. Our job, as understood by the chief on down, is to solve this crime while maintaining the status quo. Now that we're up to speed, this is where things will get interesting."

The Vega had descended the hill and was a few blocks from the edge of Waite Park, a single-story part of the city that contained two shopping centers and views of parking lots. The rents were low, and people invested their paychecks and then some in retail therapy. In a few minutes, Bayonne and Adam would arrive at Art Spencer's address.

"This is a tough one, kid. I'm sorry this is your first. Don't let this case twist your head around. Let's see this one through, see what we learn, and see if we can't start you off with a win."

"You really think we'll close this case?"

Bayonne told him his theory about how you get a sense of each murder when you first see the scene, how murders scream at you, and, through experience, you learn to understand the language of a murder, read the forensics, the body, and the scene. By the time they pulled to the curb in front of Art Spencer's red brick, flat-roofed apartment complex, his new partner thought Bayonne nuttier than a fruitcake.

"So, if you can communicate with murder scenes, what is this one telling you?"

"I didn't say I could communicate with murder scenes."

"But they communicate with you. What are you hearing?"

Bayonne knew he'd sounded like a lunatic. "Well, that's another thing about this case. I can't hear a thing."

"You don't hear anything?"

"Not word one."

"So, if I understand what you're saying, you have a power to communicate with crime scenes. You are, essentially, a super detective, but your power doesn't work on this case. Is that right?"

"Well, when you put it that way—"

"I'm not trying to put it any way. I'm just trying to understand."

"I don't communicate with crime scenes. I'm using a metaphor. I'm just saying that if you take things in, you get a feel for what happened. That's all I'm saying."

"But you don't get a feel this time."

"Nothing."

"Jesus Christ." The rookie detective ran a handful of chubby fingers through his hair.

Bayonne pointed to the eyesore Art Spencer had called home. "Maybe we'll learn something in here."

"Maybe we'll hear voices."

"We should be so lucky."

Bayonne and Adam walked down the long, gray hallway until they found the right unit, stuck crime scene tape across the door, and Bayonne used Art Spencer's key to open the lock.

The interior of the apartment was as gray, as dreary, and as depressing as the exterior and the hallway. Bayonne glanced out of the only window, a small vertical rectangle in the living room; the view consisted of a shopping mall, which could've been a school or a prison, barely visible through the limbs of a blue spruce. Talk about an aesthetic death.

Bayonne and Adam searched the place with rubber gloves on. Spencer had two fiberboard bookcases that looked like they'd been purchased at Target, a cheap leather couch, and a cheaper recliner, also probably purchased at Target. Three motivational posters showed images

of natural wonders and described the virtues of a positive attitude, ambition, and potential, respectively. His
twenty-seven-inch TV sat in a fiberboard entertainment
center. Shelves on the side contained the VCR and stereo.
Cords ran from the receiver to speakers mounted on the
wall, a pretty nice set up for a guy with no taste.

Word art framed the door to the bedroom. One
mass-produced, painted piece of birch provided syn-
onyms for success, and the other had barely survived the
ravages of a brainstorm around the word love. Bayonne
studied the two pastiches, and said, "I guess his mind
wasn't going to go to mush on its own."

"You would know."

The detectives searched for anything personal in the
bedroom, and found nothing, no family photographs,
no tchotchkes, and no sign of life. Black-and-white stock
photos of cityscapes, Paris hung over the bed and New
York hung over the chest of drawers. Half of Spencer's
closet contained argyle sweaters, tweed, and corduroy.
The other half silk shirts, Armani jackets, and designer
blue jeans. This guy either went to work to keep the youth
safe for democracy or auditioned for Miami Vice. No
middle ground.

Adam carried a large cardboard box out of the closet
and set it on the bed.

"What's this?" Bayonne asked.

"Stag films. Lots of them."

He held a VHS toward Bayonne's face, and the veteran
stared into the timeless embrace of an overweight man

and two drug-addled vixens.

"Oh, my. Our first glimpse into the true character of this math teacher."

There were numerous videos in the box, tales of love and lust, erotic adventure, and the awakening of yearning desire. They hadn't come to judge the man's predilections, not, at least, until Adam emerged from the closet with another shoe box. Adam stood next to the bed and thumbed through the contents before upending it. The photographs that fell onto the bed showed the victim with dozens of different women, women who held onto him, who smiled blissfully into the camera, who held something out to him, or looked into his face longingly, seeking the return of their emotions. None of the images were crude or even suggestive. All had been taken in public places, museums, parks, parties, weddings, and random social events. They were simple, mildly domestic, desperate, needy, each in her own way.

Bayonne picked up one of the slips of stationary interspersed with the photographs.

I haven't been able to reach you, so I thought I'd write something. Don't worry about the other night. We had a wonderful time, didn't we? I can't remember the last time I felt so good. Call me soon.

There was a little card with an image of two kittens snuggling on it.

Art, you're wonderful. It happens to every guy. I can't wait to see you again.

Bayonne handed the card to his partner and looked back

at the photographs. In each one, Art looked away, leaned away, pulled away from the woman. He often didn't look into the camera. Why did he keep them? Were these trophies? Notches on his belt? Did he get off on the desire the girls felt?

Adam said, "What happens to every guy?"

Bayonne turned around and saw his partner flipping through several notes. "Your guess is as good as mine."

A voice spoke from the doorway. "What are you doing? Why are you going through my brother's things?"

Bayonne looked up to see a woman in her early thirties, a little chubby, with chestnut bangs covering her forehead. He pulled his shield from his belt and held it out to the woman. "Did you see the police tape on the door?"

"Because you put up tape, you can go through a person's things? Do you have a warrant?"

"Miss Spencer?" Bayonne said. "Is your name Spencer?"

The woman nodded.

"Why don't you take a seat. We need to talk."

"I'd rather see your warrant."

"We don't have a warrant. That's what we need to talk to you about."

"You don't . . .?"

Miss Spencer sat on the couch and told them that her first name was Jenny. She usually spoke to her brother every day but hadn't heard from him since Saturday, so she stopped by to see if he was all right. When Bayonne told her that her brother was dead, she cried. Adam and Bayonne waited and studied the carpet.

"You were right," she said.

Bayonne said, "What were we right about, miss?"

"What you said about Art. He had a problem."

Adam asked, "What kind of problem was that?"

"What happens to every guy. He had trouble, you know . . . performing . . . with women."

Bayonne stepped into the bedroom and took a handful of the photographs from the bed. "Are you saying he didn't . . . enjoy relations with any of these women?"

"It's nineteen ninety-two. We can talk about sex. Can't we?" She said it with a laugh as she wiped her face with a tissue she'd taken from her purse. "I don't know about all of them, but a girl I set him up with spoke to me about it. She thought he might be gay, but I didn't think so. A couple of them threw it in his face when he dumped them. Once, a woman broke up with him in a restaurant with a couple of our other friends. She'd been drinking and made a scene. She said things she shouldn't have said in public."

Jenny took a deep, ragged breath. "The body language was off between him and the girls he dated. They weren't close. They didn't touch. Does that make sense? And there were so many different women, like he was trying to compensate for something or find something he didn't have. When I put it all together, I don't know, I think that was his problem."

Adam put the photographs and notes back into the box and brought the box back into the living room, setting it on the table. Bayonne thumbed through the contents of the box, lifted the Pistons cap off his head, and scratched at his hairline. "Have you ever heard of a bar called Alfie's?"

Jenny shrugged. "No. Is it here or by the college?"

Adam said, "No, it's south of Riverwalk Drive."

"I've never gone to a bar south of the river."

Bayonne said, "Did Art?"

"I don't know. He might've. He had a friend who liked to go out drinking."

"What was his friend's name?"

"Bernie Peters."

Bayonne needed a drink.

***

An hour later, Bayonne and Adam were back in Bayonne's Vega heading south.

Adam said, "The case telling you anything now?"

"Art Spencer and Bernie Peters went to college together. That's a start."

"I figured that. Maybe I have super powers, too."

Bayonne cracked his window and lit a cigarette. "You know, for a guy who gets green at the sight of a dead body, you've turned into quite the smartass."

"It's not the bodies that get me. I told you that. It's the way they're posed."

"Have you figured out what it reminds you of?"

"No. I don't know. It's like I can almost see it, and then I get sick. I can't focus on it." Adam stared out the window for a few beats. "You think Bernie Peters is the killer?"

"We've got to take a run at him, but it doesn't make sense. Why would he sit around at Mason's and get his name in the investigation when he didn't have to? He could've

taken off before we got there." Bayonne held the cigarette to the crack in the window and let the ash fly. "Okay.
How about this? Why was the guy paying prostitutes if
he couldn't get it up? That seems like a waste of money."

Adam held the shoe box of photographs in his lap and
stared out the window. "He might not have been able to
consummate a relationship with a girl he respected."

Bayonne sucked on his nail, exhaled, and raised an
eyebrow. "Is that a thing?"

"You'd be surprised. It's the type of thing we studied
in college."

"I am surprised. You don't look like a guy who studied
sex in college."

"Psychology, which has a lot to do with sex. At least
some people connect psychology to sex. In either case, I
think that's what these notes were about. I think he was
a serial dater."

"What does this have to do with breakfast?"

"A serial dater is someone who dates several women in
quick succession, enjoys the hunt in the first few dates,
but can't engage in a deep, meaningful, and lasting relationship."

"We used to call that lucky. Why did he document the
relationships? Why did he collect a shoe box full of
photographs of women he didn't sleep with?"

"Maybe, in a way, they are his trophies, reminders of his
shame, of his innocence. The photos are proof he wasn't
a horrible guy because he didn't do to them what he did
to the working girls."

"That makes him a good guy?"

"Those were women he felt deserved it. The girls in the pictures he felt didn't deserve it."

"I wonder how they felt." Bayonne scratched his beard with the hand that held his cigarette. "Why would anyone kill this guy? Even if your nickel psychology is right on. From what you saw, what would motivate someone to strangle a math teacher in a no-tell motel on the south side?"

"I don't know."

"Just take it all in for a second. This guy didn't actually do anything physical to women who weren't selling it. He took his legitimate dates to the zoo, to dinner, or to a ballgame. Their affairs were emotional, or as emotional as he could get. Maybe they would've liked him to do more. I don't know. In any case, he wasn't hurting anyone beyond stringing them along. He wasn't selling drugs or starting fights or a threat to anyone anywhere. He partied and taught eighth graders. People don't kill people just because they can't get it up. People kill people out of desire, anger, or perversion. This guy is about as devoid of extreme passions as anyone you'll find."

Adam held up an image of Art Spencer looking so bored he was about to fall asleep. The woman on his arm smiled into the camera while the man of her illusions stifled a yawn.

"If he had problems with women he respected," Adam said, "it might have made him aggressive with the girls he didn't respect. He might've gotten rough with a prost and she fought back."

"And posed his hands?" Bayonne said. "Besides, he doesn't read like someone who'd rough up a working girl."

"Hard to tell."

"Would any prost you ever busted have a problem with this guy?"

That made Adam laugh. "Is the killer a prost? Another john?"

"Maybe . . . I don't know. I have no idea why these guys were killed. Art Spencer had a problem with women he respected, but I don't know if that has anything to do with his death. Connolly was a junkie bartender, but everyone we talked to liked him."

"This could all be random."

"Do you have any idea how rare it is for someone to kill someone randomly? There's something about Alfie's and Shady Pines that we don't understand. That's the connection between three out of four murders."

Adam said, "Three johns and a bartender. Why the bartender?"

"He must've known something. He knew about Spencer. He must've made a connection we're not seeing."

"And the killer murdered Connolly because of what he knew? Why not shoot Connolly or stab him or just give him a bad dose? Why drug him, strangle him, and pose his hands? Why go to so much trouble? Why draw this much attention?"

"I don't know." Bayonne let his cigarette slide out the

crack in the window.

"We're not much closer than we were before we drove uptown."

"We connected Spencer to Bernie Peters. We've got the scent now, but there's something else. A shadow of something. Something trying to speak, but I can't hear it. I just don't know what it is, yet."

"We need to see if they've identified the two other bodies at the morgue," Adam said.

"We need to talk to Bernie Peters."

SIX

CHASING TAIL
1:12PM Thursday, September 3, 1992

The sun had passed its midpoint about an hour before, and Kane sat in his Buick Regal on the corner of Navajo and 26th. He'd just finished a sandwich and was filling a travel mug from a thermos when he saw movement in his side view. He snapped the lid on his mug with one hand and tightened the top on his Stanley with the other. A flicker of denim showed next to his Regal's bumper, someone in a jean jacket crouching alongside the car.

He pulled his Ruger, a .45, not a great gun, but cheap and relatively reliable, from the holster stuck between his seat and the center console. He opened the door and shoved the pistol into the face of a fourteen-year-old.

The fourteen-year-old smiled.

"What are you doing?"

The kid blinked at the barrel, confusing yet familiar.

"We never saw this car before, not around here."

"We?"

The chunk of concrete bounced across the hood of Kane's Regal. Like an idiot, he stood to look, and both kids were gone, nothing but a blur of denim and laughter.

The broken-down residence he'd been watching had once been the symbol of the American dream, in 1947, maybe. The house had been designed, like every other house below South Street, for the burgeoning working class during the postwar boom, when the old neighborhoods of St. Patrick's, Woodland, and Commerce City had gentrified, and swaths of hastily constructed, single-family dwellings had been thrown together to house the workers whose sweat fueled the happy days here again. The fields that had gone undeveloped were now filled with trailer parks or manufacturing plants, and the houses had weathered poorly. The Molloy house was no exception. Yellow paint, probably lead-based, hung off the wall in chunks and chips. The yard had gone to seed, and the screen door hung off its hinges, dangling over a two-foot drop where a front stoop should've been.

Crystal wasn't home. If she was working the streets, she'd be out between eleven and four. Street walkers rarely work the night shift. They work the middle of the day when businessmen don't need excuses. Even if she wasn't on the sledge, why would she hang around here? Nobody else did, no family, no guests, and no sleazy uncles. In fact, there'd been no activity at all for over an hour.

Kane drove around for a while before he found her, a young girl, seemingly apprehensive, defensive body language, and no track marks. He saw her from a block away, five-foot-four, brown hair in pig tails, a little like Diamond might've looked before the lifestyle robbed her of her best years. She wore a thick camouflage jacket, patched in two places with duct tape, over a yellow flowered sun dress, white knee highs, and men's work boots two sizes too big, and she stood on the corner with a leg extended, kicking at the curb's edge, like she was trying to show a little sex appeal but didn't know how.

Despite the camouflage, she stuck out like a sore thumb on the south side, a difficult neighborhood for the most seasoned veteran. Three girls, whose neon pink or yellow winter coats set them off from the brick wall they leaned against, kept their distance from the kid they watched. Their leathered, blotched skin and off-the-rack wigs gave them the appearance of a heavy metal band, and they weren't ready to compete with or encourage the child whose strange presence made them wary about their choices and hesitant about hers. By the end of the week, they would've found in her an angle to play.

Kane pulled to the curb, rolled down his window, gave her his biggest, most guileless smile, and waved her over.

She leaned on the window like it was a life raft and said, "You looking for a good time, honey?"

"I sure am, but I've never done this kind of thing before. Do you think you could help me out?"

"You're not a cop, are you? You've got to tell me if you are."

Kane knew that wasn't actually true. A cop didn't have to identify himself or herself in the middle of a sting, but television has a way of giving people funny ideas. In any case, Kane told the truth. "I'm not a cop, darling. I don't even like cops."

She opened the door and slid into the passenger seat. "I don't like cops, either. They're the worst kind of customers."

"Do you know somewhere we could go?"

"I've got a flop over on Division Street, if you want to take the drive. The room costs extra."

Kane drove a couple of blocks in silence before pulling over and hitting the power locks. She looked at him like he'd kicked her dog.

"What are you doing? Why are we stopping?"

"I'm not a john, Crystal. You know the big Polish guy, Seth? He works with Diamond at The Side Saddle."

"What about him?"

"He sent me. He wanted to do Diamond a favor. He's trying to look out for Di and her family."

She was silent for a minute. When she spoke, she was sixteen going on fifty. "Why would he do that? He only met me once."

"I think Amber had something to do with it."

"That makes sense. Amber's a flake, but she's got a good heart. I've known her for years. She and my sister were in high school together."

The girl took out a cigarette, and Kane cracked the window and lit it for her. She exhaled a cloud.

"Your sister hit a bit of a rough patch."

"Her whole life is a rough patch. Di's too much like my mom."

"And you're not? It seems like you're following in your sister's footsteps."

She ran her wrist under her nose and held it there. "Look, if you want to talk, I still need forty dollars."

"Forty dollars? For a friendly conversation?"

"Is that what this is? Aren't you going to try me out? See if I'm good enough to work at The Saddle? You can't fool me."

Kane thought about this for a minute. She wasn't asking an outrageous price. She wasn't experienced enough to try to set a high point from which to negotiate. She didn't expect this to go anywhere. She thought herself a mark but wasn't above setting the stakes. Forty struck Kane as an odd number.

"What do you need forty for? What are you doing out here?"

"My mom's sick. She needs medicine."

"How old are you?"

"Eighteen."

Eighteen that'll get you twenty. Kane pulled a wad of bills out of his pocket and let her get a good look at it. He set two twenties on his lap, watched her eyes follow them, and stuffed the wad back into his jeans, where it belonged around this jailbait, while keeping a hand on the two twenties.

"I'm not here to turn you out. I'm here to help if I can, if you'll let me."

She stared at the money for a few ticks, and her eyes flicked toward his pocket, where he'd shoved the wad of bills.

"Look, why don't we go see your mom? Maybe we can help her. I bet I can get her the medicine she needs. Maybe I can help you, too. If you let me help you, I'll kick you the forty. What do you think?"

"If I take you to see my mom, will you give me a job?"

"We can talk about a job."

"You seem like a cop or something."

"I'm the furthest thing from a cop. Maybe I'm something."

Kane started the car and whipped a u. He parked in front of her house, a hundred yards from where he'd parked earlier.

"She's not like us. She's not for sale, not like that."

"Your mom? Like what, then?"

"She's got a problem."

"The needle? Is she inside?"

"She never leaves."

When Kane stepped from the car, he glanced around for those two kids. He didn't know what he would find inside the house, and he wanted to be ready for anything, so he slid the Ruger into his pants behind his back and stuffed the two twenties into a back pocket.

"Hey, I thought that was mine."

She didn't mention the gun.

"It will be. Show me, and don't yank me around."

"I can yank you off for three of those twenties, if you want?"

The price went up. She saw Kane as a mark now, not a

john, someone trying to help a lost cause, an idiot, which was more accurate than thinking him a cop. She learned fast. Kane pulled his black leather jacket from the back seat to cover the pistol.

"Watch your mouth. We're going to see your mother."

"She doesn't give a shit."

Kane followed her to the door. She lifted up a pot, whatever had been growing in the dust long since dead, and pulled a key from underneath. Kane rolled his eyes behind her back. She unlocked the door and stepped inside. The stank of mold and diarrhea hit him in the face. Kane gagged and leaned out the open door.

"This isn't pretty."

In that moment, she looked twelve, just a kid in a world that knew how to turn you against yourself.

"Take me to her."

She led the way down a dark hall and opened the door to what would have been the master bedroom, had anything like a master ever lived in this rundown, rotting firetrap. A woman sprawled on the bed, the sheets soaked in sweat and incontinence, and the blanket tossed onto the floor. Two syringes, a spoon, and a book of matches sat on the nightstand next to an empty bottle of Silver Wolf vodka. A porcelain lamp hadn't put up much of a fight when it had shattered against the wall. The woman was still breathing, but she only mumbled and rolled over, coughing and farting before losing consciousness.

"Does your phone work?"

"We don't have a phone."

"When was the last time you ate?"

They sat in silence during the ten-minute drive up to Commerce City. Kane thought over what he'd seen. Did Crystal's mom even know how far she'd fallen? He'd seen a lot of people destroy themselves over the years. Some people do it in a year or two. Other people need decades. Two years ago, Diamond had been a fun-loving party girl. Now, at twenty-two or twenty-three, she looked more like her mom than her sister. They'd lost hope, he thought, or maybe they'd just lost their bearings. Whatever had once given them the strength in the morning to rise and give the day a puncher's chance had now faded into a distorted memory, a hallucination misted over by a thousand lies they'd told themselves to feel a little less guilty or embarrassed or broken by the piling up of bad decisions.

Kane glanced at the teenager next to him, definitely a few decisions down the wrong road.

He pulled into the parking lot of a McDonald's where he bought her a Happy Meal, which he hoped lived up to its name. While she ate, Kane used the phone outside to page Detective Bayonne. When Bayonne called back, Kane told him about the situation, and he said he'd need a few minutes to set things up. Kane hung up and called St. Catherine's while watching the girl through the window. She picked up the plastic robot that had come with her lunch, looked at it, and tossed it onto the table. Finding a better toy, she fished a cigarette out of her pack and lit it. Kane gave his name and asked the matronly voice on the other end to transfer him to Father Nick. The line clicked without so much as a word.

"Kane Kulpa, as I live and breathe."

"How are you, Father Nick?"

"It is I who should be asking you that question, son."

"I need a favor."

Kane explained the situation to the man who'd once offered him a home when he'd had none. Father Nick listened without interrupting, and when Kane finished, said, "Who will pay for her place here?"

"I'll pay what the church won't."

"Where did your money come from? We heard about the trial. We prayed for you."

Kane didn't know what to say, so he let that pass. "Will you help her? She's got nobody."

"Who do you have, Kane? Who's helping you?"

"If you do this, you would be."

Kane could hear him hold the receiver away from his mouth as he coughed. He'd smoked two packs a day when Kane had known him.

"Will you be bringing her here today?"

"Once I drop off the mother, I'll be by."

"I won't be here this afternoon, but I'll leave instructions for Miss Garcia. She will help you process the paperwork through social services. The church will cover the girl's stay."

Kane hung up, caught his breath, and turned back to the young girl beyond the glass. He didn't need to think over how to convince her. Either the direct approach would work or nothing.

Sitting in the booth across from her, he asked, "Has your mom ever gone to rehab?"

"Twice, when she got her DUIs. She didn't used to be this bad. She only drank and smoked pot, but after she lost her license the second time, about a year ago, she lost her job at the paint factory. She couldn't get to work on time."

"Did Diamond help you out?"

"No, she'd been gone over a year then. She swore she'd never be like Mom."

"What happened to your mom after she lost her job?"

"She got a check on the first and fifteenth. She worked part time washing dishes at Lou's for cash, but she got fired. I think she went to work drunk."

"So, you're out here trying to help your mom."

"For a smart guy, you're not too bright. There's no helping Mom. You want to help? I need some cash."

"What are you doing, then? Why are you on the sledge?"

"You want me to wash dishes? Mix paint chemicals? What do you think I'm going to do? I need to put together a down payment."

"What for?"

"So I can hustle. You need to buy in if you want to hustle."

"What are you talking about? Hustle?"

"You said you could get my mom medicine. I want as much medicine as I can get my hands on. I've already got a bit saved up. If you help me get some smack, I'll make it worth your while. People will do anything to get that stuff, and I want to be the one who gets it for them."

Kane wondered if he had talked that way once. He didn't

think he had ever been so naïve. She didn't know what she was talking about, but she wasn't entirely wrong, either. He hoped he'd changed over the years, become someone else. But he couldn't swear he was so different from the reality of the person she hoped to become.

"You don't feel bad?" he said. "The brown ruined your mom's life. You want to ruin other people's?"

"Nobody worried about me. Why should I worry about them?"

Kane heard the phone ringing outside and hustled through the double doors to answer it. Detective Bayonne told him he'd gotten her into a rehab program for informants and gave him an address for an inpatient clinic in Woodland Park.

"I owe you one, Vinnie."

"After the Connolly mess, you owe me a couple, and don't think I ain't keeping track, but it sounds like you're doing a good thing. I'm glad I could help."

On the drive back to her house, Kane tried a different approach. "My mom went through rehab a couple times."

Crystal watched and waited for his play. "Yeah? How's she doing now?"

"She's got problems. I try to take care of her, but she's sick. She can't work a good job anymore."

Crystal stared out the window. "That's too bad."

"Sometimes I can hear her voice, you know? But it isn't her now. It's her old voice, the way she sounded when I was a kid. I'm not even sure I remember it right. It might just be my voice or something I made up, but it speaks to me."

"What does it say?"

"It tells me things are okay, things I know aren't okay."

"What does that mean?"

"The voice encourages the worst part of me. It encourages me to be weak, to get angry, to feed my hunger. When I'm weighing two options, the voice tells me to take the easy road, even if I know that's the wrong choice."

Crystal didn't say anything.

"Do you know what I mean?"

"Maybe."

Kane didn't have anything else to say, so he sat in silence.

A few ticks passed, and Crystal said, "I think I've got you figured out."

"How's that?"

"You want to be loved."

"Doesn't everybody?"

"Not like you. You want the real deal, nothing held back."

She might've been smarter than Kane had given her credit for.

"You need to learn that it's not about the love you want," she said. "It's about the love you get."

"Where'd you learn that?"

"It was on a trick's bumper sticker. The guy drove last year's Cadillac but only paid sixty bucks. He said it was all he had. I figured he knew a thing or two about getting stuff."

"Is that where you learned how to get?"

"One of the places."

"Will you let me take your mom to rehab?"

"It's about the only thing for her, but who's paying for it?"

"She'll go in as an informant. The cops will pay."

Crystal laughed at that.

Kane had to carry the mother wrapped in a blanket to his car, doing his best to keep her bodily fluids contained in the blanket and not on his backseat. She woke up briefly, cursed at him and at her daughter, and passed the fuck back out. Kane didn't say anything, but Crystal started to cry.

Kane carried the mother into the clinic and helped Crystal fill out the paperwork. While they walked back to the car, she looked a whiter shade of pale. She said, "Why are you doing this?"

"I told you. Seth asked me to."

"Do you do everything he asks? Are you his slave?"

Kane stopped in the middle of the parking lot and turned toward her. She took a step back, like he was going to hit her, and she wiped both her cheeks with her right hand, one after the other.

"Listen, Seth and I have been friends a long time, and we've seen a lot of people like your mother. I've seen some get better and some get worse. I know what it does to a family, and I know, whether you like it or not, you need to help others when you can, at least a little."

"Do you sell what made her sick?"

"I'm not a pusher."

She stared at him, and Kane thought she knew he wasn't that far removed. He looked away, and said, "People aren't just one thing."

"Who are you?"

"My name is Kane. I'm not a good man. Don't misread the situation."

"Then why are you trying to help? I think you are, actually, trying to help."

"There's a first time for everything. Do you know St. Catherine's?"

"The reform school? Everybody does."

"I know a priest there. He said he would take you in. There will be other kids your age there, girls and boys. I don't want you living on your own. This will keep you off the street. Is that okay with you?"

"Do I still get the forty?"

Some things never change.

"Sure, but I'll give it to Father Nick and he'll put it in an account for you. Does that work?"

"How about you give me twenty and give him the other twenty."

SEVEN

A MAN WITH TWO FIRST NAMES

3:47PM Thursday, September 3, 1992

Bayonne felt good until he and Adam got north of downtown. He'd never liked The Heights. Most of the houses looked the same, ostentatious doppelgangers for people who lived ostentatious lives mirroring the lives of their neighbors. The place felt like a labyrinth, the solution to which was an examined life, Bayonne assumed. He and Adam had to turn around twice in cul-de-sacs and retrace their route back to a numbered street before they found the Peters' residence.

Bayonne whistled at the sight of the place.

Adam raised an eyebrow. "This is all it takes to impress you?"

Blue spruce and cedars framed the two-story red brick neocolonial. Palladian windows glared from either side of the pediment-topped portico. Bayonne parked in the driveway, and the two detectives followed the cobblestone around the rose bushes to the doorbell. Mrs. Peters opened the door and presented an image of domestic tranquility. She wore a sweater paired with tan slacks. Her makeup was light but strategic, and blond highlights gave her dirty blond-feathered-do an effervescent glow.

"Detectives Bayonne and McKenna. Thank you for coming."

It felt nice to be treated so nicely, but Bayonne wasn't sure why she thanked them. They hadn't been invited.

Bayonne had passed the word through dispatch to have radio cars looking for Bernie Peters as a person of interest in four homicides. If a unit found him, they were to call in the location and maintain surveillance. Bayonne and Adam had taken a closer look at Bernie and learned he was a successful real estate developer without a criminal record.

"As I said on the phone, my husband isn't here at the moment. I don't know where he is."

"We understand that, Mrs. Peters," Bayonne said. "We were hoping to speak with you anyway, if you don't mind."

"Of course. Please, take a seat in the sitting room."

Made sense.

Tables overflowing with plastic flowers and porcelain miniatures had been set against each wall in the entry-way. The place was like a mine field. As he navigated the corners, Bayonne's coat caught a porcelain puppy, which shattered against the Red Oak floor. He apologized, but

Mrs. Peters shrugged it off, saying she should've offered to take his coat, and the figure needed replacing anyway. Need seemed a strong word.

To hide his amusement, Adam turned toward the picture window looking out over the manicured backyard. He said, "You have a wonderful home here, Mrs. Peters."

"Thank you."

She ran her hands beneath her slacks as she sat.

Bayonne absent-mindedly took the tin from his back pocket and began to flick it between his thumb and forefinger, thought better of it, and stuffed it into his jacket pocket.

"So, you are aware, Mrs. Peters, you are speaking to two police officers. You are under no obligation to provide evidence against your husband."

"Against my husband? Has he done something? Is he under suspicion?"

Bayonne raised his hands, palms outward. "We just want to cover all the bases. We want you to know who you are talking to and to feel at ease."

"That was an odd way to put me at ease."

It was at this point that Adam stepped in. The guy was new, but he had a way with the northside set.

"What my partner is trying to say, Mrs. Peters, is that we want to ask a few questions, but you are under no obligation to answer. If you feel that our questions require you to incriminate your husband in any way, you need not respond. That said, murder has been committed, and we would appreciate your cooperation. We will be as discreet as possible, and anything that doesn't need to become public knowledge won't be. That includes your and your husband's involvement. We'll do our best to keep personal information out of our official reports. Do you understand what I am saying to you?"

The broad looked from one detective to the other, the youthful, out-of-shape nerd on one side and the grizzled, nicotine-stained veteran on the other.

She smiled. "You're saying that your discretion will increase in proportion to my cooperation. The two of you are an interesting pair."

Adam, straight as an arrow, said, "As you may or may not know, your husband was at a house where a man was found dead in St. Patrick's Diocese the night of August thirty-first, into the morning of the first of September. Do you know why he was there?"

Every ounce of warmth disappeared from her eyes, two drops of sapphire in a meticulously sculpted face. "My husband has appetites, hungers, if you will, and he chases them wherever they lead. I'm not sure how much he can control and how much he can't anymore. Perhaps his drives control him, but you see that all the time on the television, don't you? That's just how the world is, I think."

"With that in mind, what, specifically, was your husband doing in St. Patrick's?"

She snorted. "He was getting high and probably having sex with some whore or two or three."

Bayonne snorted. "And you're okay with that?"

She turned her gaze on Bayonne, and for a moment he

thought he might be chased from the house, and then the corners of her mouth turned up.

"I understand your question, and no, I'm not. My husband and I have lived separate lives for several years, but the money was mine, from my father. I inherited the money Bernie used to start his firm. I didn't know him well enough when we were married, or maybe he changed, or I did, but he is who he is. And if I left him, he'd get half of everything, half my family's wealth."

Bayonne considered the man he'd briefly spoken to outside of Mason's. Bernie's wasn't a confidence born of wealth. His was the confidence of a sneak thief, someone who thought he could pull one over on anyone.

Adam gave Bayonne a look to keep his mouth shut before he continued. "Have you known your husband to go to any specific bars or clubs, places in St. Patrick's or Commerce City, perhaps?"

"I don't know where exactly he goes. I've seen matchbooks from time to time, and cocktail napkins with phone numbers on them. He's gone to places called The Side Saddle, The Red Carpet, and The Hassle House. I didn't know there were bars like that until after we were married."

Adam gave nothing away. "Have you ever heard of a bar known as Alfie's?"

"Never."

"Do you know any of the people your husband associates with in the evenings? Have you heard specific names or ever met anyone from the south side?"

"Associates with? I'm afraid not."

"Have you ever spoken with anyone on the phone?"

"I don't know what you're searching for here, Detective. I've never been a part of that part of Bernie's life."

Adam asked, "Did you know a man named Art Spencer?"

"*Did I?*"

Adam glanced at Bayonne, and Bayonne shrugged. The rookie had flubbed that question, and Mrs. Peters had her antennae on high alert.

"Yes," Adam said. "Mr. Spencer's body was found yesterday morning."

"First this guy in St. Patrick's, and now Art? Is that why you're here?"

Bayonne said, "Your husband was a good friend of Mr. Spencer's, wasn't he?"

"We went to college with Art. We both did. I can't believe he's dead."

Mrs. Peters put a hand over her mouth and blinked several times. Bayonne watched her and wondered if she was trying to figure for herself what was going on. She appeared less distraught than shocked. When she removed the hand from her mouth, she swallowed and took a deep breath. "Art was a good man. He followed Bernie everywhere. I know Bernie got him in trouble, but it wasn't Art's fault."

Adam opened his mouth to speak, and Bayonne flicked a hand toward him, motioning him to silence.

Mrs. Peters stood and walked over to a cart in the corner and began to mix herself a drink. She didn't offer the detectives anything. "If I'd been smarter, I'd have married

Art. He wasn't the type of man who would give a girl trouble. He was smart, responsible, but simple. Bernie, though, Bernie was something else. He was fun and wild, and when we were twenty, he was very handsome. When we first started dating, we were both a little wild. He was seeing other women. I grew out of my wildness, but he didn't. I thought I was creating memories, living life to the fullest. I only realized later how self-absorbed I'd been. The memories I'd created I wished I could forget. Bernie was different. He was never going to change. As he got older, he lost his looks, and he'd never been a particularly good lover. He was, quite simply, terribly confident. It wasn't until we'd been married ten years that I realized he didn't actually care about anyone else. He only cared about himself. He doesn't see other people, I don't think. Not really. They're not real to him. Only his thoughts are real, his emotions. That's the terrible truth about Bernie Peters.

"When I realized the mistakes I'd made, I organized a charity to develop some of the housing areas in SOCCs. I wanted to do something positive with our wealth. Bernie demanded the charity be named after him. He said he wouldn't sign off on the money if it didn't carry his name. The foundation made Bernie a slum lord."

"Peters Built Housing is named after Bernie Peters?" Bayonne asked.

"I had a tubal ligation a month later. I wouldn't let him bring another Bernie into this world."

"Did he know about that?"

"He never asked. I told him I was visiting my sister, and

he never noticed I was recuperating from the procedure. He doesn't notice a lot of things." She stared out the window for a moment. "I wanted something real in my life. Now I think it's too late."

She said that Bernie had grown more and more brutal in bed. He'd started by spanking, which led to choking. He'd once beat her until she lost consciousness. They never slept together again, and Bernie often didn't come home. She'd met with Bernie's business partner a few months back and discovered that Bernie had been missing work, and his partner had been running things for almost a year.

Bernie Peters had slipped off the rails.

Adam said, "When was the last time you saw your husband?"

"Yesterday morning. He didn't go out Tuesday night, and he had a cup of coffee with me before leaving the house."

"Yesterday?" Bayonne asked. "He didn't come home last night?"

"That isn't uncommon, I'm afraid."

"Does Bernie ever use smack?"

"Not with me. When we were younger, that wouldn't have been something he would've touched. But now? I don't know. I never thought he was as much a slave to his addictions as he was a slave to being on the edge. He needed to feel as though he were in control but could lose that control at any moment."

"But you think he is losing control?"

"I think it's inevitable."

"Did Bernie have anything against Art Spencer?"

"Not that I know of. Art was a follower. He followed Bernie around. Bernie wouldn't hurt him."

Mrs. Peters gave Adam as detailed an account as she could as to her whereabouts on the nights in question. She told him what she knew of her husband's actions, which amounted to approximations of when he left the house and when he returned.

Mrs. Peters led the detectives to Bernie's office. They found a book of matches from The Side Saddle on his desk. Photographs of Bernie and local celebrities, mayors and city councilmen past and present, actors and athletes who'd grown up in the city, the entire Spirits team, and the local weatherman, hung in a spiral pattern on either side of a large bookshelf. Football and wrestling trophies filled the bookshelf, which reached almost to the ceiling. Most of the trophies were from high school and college, a few from middle school, and none more significant than a regional title. There were no images of or references to his wife.

"I'm going to make some coffee. Would either of you like a cup?"

Both detectives said they would, and Mrs. Peters disappeared. Presumably she kept a kitchen somewhere on the grounds.

Adam leaned into Bayonne and spoke in a low voice. "Does that look like a dick to you?"

"Are you suggesting that the photographs are in the shape of a pair of testicles and the bookshelf is a phallus?"

"That is what I am suggesting."

"You've got a problem."

"I've got a problem? This guy had one fucked up Rorschach Test on his wall."

"Would Art Spencer have passed that Rorschach?"

"You don't pass those. They're used to—"

"You know what I'm saying."

"You're saying it's all for show, just like Art Spencer's. There's nothing personal here, nothing that gives a sense of who he is or what his values are."

Bayonne raised an eyebrow. "You think this guy has values?"

"I think everyone has values. Some people value horrible things, the destruction of others, or their own superiority. Bernie's only sense of purpose is his own greatness."

"You think he consciously or subconsciously depicted his value on that wall in the shape of a giant penis?"

"I think he wants people to think he's a giant dick, but he's actually lost and empty, like Spencer was, each living in their own personal hells. I think Peters takes his emptiness out on others. Spencer took it out on himself."

"I'm not sure how much your college education was worth." Bayonne thought for a moment, but he couldn't hear the case. He couldn't put his finger on it. "Now that you've seen this and met the wife, do you think Bernie killed Spencer?"

"Why would he? He's the type of guy who needs someone following him, not the type of guy who kills someone following him. I don't see it, but stranger things can happen."

Bayonne glanced toward the empty hallway before he picked a locked drawer in Bernie's desk. Inside, he found several photographs of Bernie at wild parties. Among those photos, he found a few images of Art Spencer and more than a few of Mrs. Peters. He spread the photos out on the top of the desk, and he and Adam examined how the other half lived.

Adam said, "What do you think of Mrs. Peters now?"

Bayonne's hands roamed over the photographs, touching the corners to straighten the images. "I don't know. She probably knows more than she's letting on, but not much. Maybe a few names he let slip here or there or things she heard him say. She has a wilder side, no doubt, but these were taken years ago. Can you imagine her hanging out with Jimmy Mason and his girls or swilling beer at Alfie's? That's a whole other world. I can't even see her having a conversation with the Bernie Peters we met. How much is she really going to know? I bet this is a waste of time."

"She's married to the guy. Whether we can picture it or not, they have conversations. I wouldn't trust her for a heartbeat."

Bayonne's pager, clipped to his belt, began to beep. He glanced at the number, saw it was the station, and raised his eyebrows at his partner. Bayonne stepped into the labyrinth to see if he could find a phone.

"Mrs. Peters?"

Bayonne's voice echoed down the hall, bouncing off the hardwood floor and vaulted ceiling. He found her leaning against a counter, the coffee dripping at her elbow, her head in her hands. She shook as she tried to take deep breaths.

"Mrs. Peters, I've received a page. Do you think I could use your phone?"

"You think my husband is a monster, don't you? I've tried to convince myself that people are just that way. That most people are that way. But they aren't, are they?"

"No, Mrs. Peters. They are not."

"Why is he that way? Is it me? Is there something wrong with me?"

Bayonne didn't have a clue what he was doing. It had been a long time since he'd had a sensitive conversation with a woman. He thought about what Adam had said. He tried to see her for what she was, but all he saw was a beautiful, wounded woman. He acted from instinct and took a step toward her. Her face was frozen in anguish, those high cheekbones flushed and streaked by fleeing mascara.

"I've seen a lot of people struggle with addiction, Mrs. Peters, a lot of lives ruined because people couldn't help themselves. Some people just don't know what they have until it's gone."

Bayonne could feel the heat emanating from her body. She put a hand on his shoulder and slid the hand to the zipper on his coat, and she twisted the denim fabric in her fist. Something cold crept into her eyes. "You find me attractive, don't you, Detective?"

"I beg your pardon, ma'am?"

"I can tell that you do." She placed her other hand on her

upper chest, where, had her sweater been low cut, the French would have delicately identified the décolletage. Bayonne, detective that he was, deduced a surgeon's hand in the full figure's sum. She said, "I did this for my husband. I changed myself to look like the girls he chased. I wanted him to look at me the way you are looking at me now."

Bayonne didn't know how he was looking at her, but he assumed he looked pretty stupid. His hand drifted to the pack of smokes in his front shirt pocket, and the side of his palm graced the hand of Mrs. Peters.

She pulled her hand away. "I'm sorry."

Bayonne offered her a cigarette. "Nothing to apologize for."

She accepted the smoke, and he lit it for her and lit his own. His hand shook.

"Are you cold, Detective Bayonne?"

"Nervous," he said. "I haven't been that nervous in a while."

"You're not used to women, are you, Detective?"

"I guess I've gotten out of the habit, but I don't know how a man would ever get used to a woman as beautiful as you."

She smiled, and they took turns flicking ash into the sink.

"I know for a fact that it isn't your fault," Bayonne said. "Nothing you could've done made you deserve a man like that."

"Don't be too sure. Sometimes I think I was too cold. If I could've loved him the way he needed to be loved .... I don't know...."

"It isn't a way to be loved that he needs. He's chasing his own tail. That's all there is to it. He can't catch it, doesn't have the reach."

"I think he's begun to hate himself," she said. "I think he's been doing things to try to destroy himself." She swallowed her disgust. "He started to go to a club in Waite Park, a place called The Dungeon. I don't know where it is, but he was drunk a couple of weeks ago and he told me about it. He told me that those were the women I'd driven him to, deformed women. Women who'd lost their souls. He told me he'd lost his soul."

They stood a few inches apart and listened to the hall clock tick, the horrible indifference of a difficult truth volleying between them. Bayonne could smell her breath, a mixture of the morning's coffee, the tobacco massaging her lungs, and the bitter pill she'd swallowed. Bayonne was scared of the carnivorous look she'd had in her eyes and the shame and pain he'd felt. Bayonne knew it hadn't been about him. She'd responded from habit. She'd felt his desire, which could've been any man's desire, and responded to it so she could feel how she needed to feel. Bayonne knew he shouldn't dismiss what he'd seen.

"Do you mind if I use your phone, Mrs. Peters?"

"Yes. Yes, of course. There's one right here. I'll take a cup of coffee to your partner."

She turned on the faucet, put her cigarette beneath it, tossed the butt in a garbage can beneath the sink, and took the pot off the maker and set it on a hot pad on a tray with cream, sugar, and three mugs. Bayonne, assuming there was no need for pretense, watched the heart shape sealed in her slacks as she disappeared into the hall. Bernie Peters was some kind of moron.

***

Bayonne and Adam didn't speak until Bayonne was spinning the wheel on his Vega, trying to get out of another cul-de-sac. He may have muttered a curse beneath his breath.

"Do you want me to drive?"

"Not on your life." Bayonne lowered his window a crack and lit a smoke.

"You really hate it up here, don't you?"

"I don't hate it. It just isn't me. I grew up in a working-class neighborhood in northwest Detroit, spent three years in Vietnam, and then became a cop. I grew up around the people we serve, protect, and arrest. I fought with the same type. It's all I've ever known."

Rain Dogs reached the end of side two, and the cassette clicked over. The volume had been turned low because Bayonne had gotten the impression his partner was not a Tom Waits fan.

"What was the page about? Did they ID the two John Does?"

"The desk sergeant got a strange call today. We're going to have to do an interview tonight."

"Why'd he call you?"

Bayonne flicked ash out the slit above his window. "He recognized the description."

"*You* know the guy?"

"A few years ago, I put him away for felony possession with an attempt to distribute. That's why I want you to run the interview."

"Bad blood?"

"No, I don't think so. I just want to be sure we get every-thing here we need. I don't want my past to influence the questions we ask."

Adam stared out the side window and watched the sprinklers paint rainbows in the clean, white-collar air.

"You did good work in there," Bayonne said. "You knew how to talk to her. I didn't. You knew when to take the lead. That's good work."

The downtown skyline hung on the right, and Bayonne turned the volume up a little in an attempt to discourage discussion. He sucked on the nail and exhaled out of the left side of his mouth.

"You did a good job comforting her in the kitchen."

"You were eavesdropping?"

Adam chuckled. "Not exactly. I followed you into the hall to help find a phone, and when I heard her crying, I thought I'd linger."

"I knew you were a lingerer. You know, that would've been a good time to give your partner backup."

"I didn't want to put myself in the line of fire."

"It wasn't a real advance."

"It sure as hell sounded real."

Bayonne shivered, dragged on his smoke, exhaled, and took a deep breath. "I'm not sure what it was."

"I do. She was using offense as her best defense. We were cops in her house investigating her husband. We were a threat but not a sexual threat. I think that's how she handles threats. That may be why she was drawn to Bernie Peters. She may have meant to create a distraction or to exert power or release tension. It might've been instinctual or done on purpose. I'm guessing it was all of that. It's who she is."

Bayonne thought about this a few beats. "When I meet a woman like that, a beautiful, intelligent, well-off woman who derives her self-worth from the opinions of men and her sense of vitality from her ability to manipulate, I worry about all of us."

"You've got one hell of a blind spot. Would you feel the same way if she weren't a knockout? She didn't have to live that way. She could've married someone else."

"True, but you and I both sized her up from her neck to her knees. Are we examples of someone else?"

"We're better than Bernie Peters."

"In some ways, sure. Obviously. In other ways, I wonder."

"You don't think we're better than some two-timing piece of shit who pays junkies to get him off?"

"I think we've all got the same urges. You and I don't act on them like a couple of degenerates, at least as far as I know, but there isn't as much distance between us and Bernie as I wish there were."

A couple blocks passed, and Tom Waits growled softly at the two policemen.

Adam said, "You know I went to St. Benedict's, a boarding school in Chicago."

"How would I know that?"

"You read my file when the captain assigned me as

your partner."

"Maybe I did."

"When I first went to St. Ben's, I had a hard time connecting to people. I thought everyone was privileged, stuck up, didn't know how to work for anything. I wore my working-class identity like a suit of armor. It took me about a year to realize that I was the one who had the problem. I was the one who felt insecure and needed to change in order to make friends and find my way."

"Are you trying to tell me that I need to change?"

"I'm saying you're a good man, and you did a good thing in there. And maybe I'm saying you're right. It's easy to amplify people's faults, to judge them for the choices they've made. It's hard to see the parallels between who they are and who you are. It's hard to feel humbled by other people's problems."

Bayonne wasn't sure that was what he'd said, and he wasn't sure where, exactly, Adam was going with this, so he didn't say anything.

Adam said, "It's a balance, isn't it?"

"What is?"

"Knowing how to work some people and help other people without losing a sense of who you are. Knowing how to be decent without losing desires, losing passion. She played the victim, and we let her because we objectified her. For all we know, she could be part of this thing. She sure as shit knows more about her husband than she wanted to admit."

"You think she still parties with Bernie?"

"I think she's got a wilder side than she wanted us to know. We saw it in those pictures you found in Bernie's desk."

Bayonne shook his head. "They were taken years ago. She hadn't even had surgery then. Nothing connects her to any of the murders other than her husband and that she knew Art Spencer. We have no reason to think she's messed up in this thing. As far as we know, she's just a woman in pain." Bayonne took a long drag and exhaled. "Hang in there, kid. You already know it's a balancing act. That's more than I knew at your age. Just watch out for the porcelain puppies."

That got a smile out of Adam, and they crossed the river into Woodland Park, which got a smile out of Bayonne.

EIGHT

DOGS EAT DOGS

5:07PM Thursday, September 3, 1992

Kane stood behind the bar, elbow-deep in dishwater, a rag in one hand and a pint glass in the other. Bruno sat at the bar with a fella who went by the name Skeet. Only a degenerate would ever self-apply a nickname, especially one that referred to ejaculate, and Skeet, a degenerate of the lowest order, had a lowlife's way of doing things.

Skeet sucked his Seven and Seven through a tiny straw and, after each sip, gulped air like he was drowning. Between gasps he turned to Bruno, and said, "I came straight from The Spanish Fly."

"Take it easy. Don't get jammed up."

"I saw the poor bastard after it happened. Naked as the day he was born and curled up like a praying baby. Hands folded and everything."

"You saw him?"

"For real. He had his belt wrapped around his neck."

Bruno glanced at Kane and caught Kane watching. "What were you doing there?"

Skeet, the specter of transience discarded for more pleasant memories, gave Bruno a grin full of yellow teeth. "I stopped by The Fly to check up on Stacey. You know, the redhead with the big tits. That girl's got healing hands."

"What were you doing looking at the body?"

Skeet blinked a couple times. "Stacey didn't seem to mind. What was I supposed to look at?"

"Not that body. The dead guy."

"Oh, I'd just finished my massage and was in the hall, on my way out, when I heard the scream. I turned around and there he was on the floor in a room. The schoolgirl found him."

"A schoolgirl?"

"Yeah. Sheila, the one who always wears a Catholic schoolgirl uniform."

Bruno looked around the room. "Did you see who did it?"

"Nobody got a good look at him. People mind their own business in those places. You know that." Skeet swallowed hard. "He was like a ghost, in and out. Nobody saw anything suspicious."

"How many people were there? Was it a packed house?"

"It's hard to say, you know. The hallway is dark, and they keep the doors closed to the rooms whether they're in use or not. There weren't many girls up front, so maybe it was pretty busy."

"Who was he?"

"I told you, I didn't see the guy." Skeet sucked on his drink.

"The john. You said you saw him in all his glory. Who was he? What did the john look like?"

"I don't know. Average. Uncircumcised, if that makes a difference to you."

"Skeet, I don't give a fuck about his dick. Who was he?"

"I never met him before. Andrews thought he knew him. Bart or Bert or something. I think he had two first names."

Bruno nodded and stared into his gin and tonic. He frowned and slid the low ball toward Kane. The glass was still half full or half empty, depending on your perspective. Kane wiped his hands on a towel and pulled Bruno's gin from the top shelf.

The heavy wooden door slid open and the daylight shrouded the face of Tae Yoon Lee who wore a suit and topcoat. Tae nodded to Bruno and walked to the far end of the bar.

Kane set Bruno's drink in front of him.

The phone rang, and Kane lifted the receiver to his ear, listened for a few seconds, and turned to Bruno.

"It's Andrews. He wants to know what to do."

"You mind taking care of that?" Bruno put a mitt on the skeeze's shoulder and squeezed, a show of friendship and strength. "Thanks for coming in, Skeet. If you see anything else or hear anything, you let me know, and the drinks are on the house."

Kane left the phone off the hook and took a Styrofoam cup from beneath the bar. He held the cup up so Skeet could see it. "You want one for the road, Skeet?"

Skeet looked around at the empty bar, frowned, and looked into Bruno's face, hovering near his shoulder. "Oh, yeah. Sure. I've got to be going."

Kane mixed a Seven and Seven in the Styrofoam cup, put a lid on it, a straw in it, and handed it to Skeet, who drained his glass and rubbed out his cigarette.

"Thanks, guys. I'll stop by when I know something else."

Bruno nodded. "Always a pleasure."

Skeet stumbled backward, and for a moment he looked like he was going to be sick. Skeet swallowed his nausea and gave Kane and Bruno a good look at his yellow teeth. He nodded and swung his shoulder into the door, head down as he left.

Bruno turned to Tae Yoon Lee. "Something to drink?"

"Guinness."

Kane pulled a pint, handed it to Bruno, and picked up the phone.

Bruno nodded to Kane, lifted his glass and the pint, and walked over to sit with Tae.

Kane watched the two men for a few beats before turning his back to them and speaking into the phone. "Andrews, get everybody out and tell them they didn't see anything. They weren't there. I'm afraid you and the girl need to stay. Detective Bayonne will be out."

Andrews spoke in a falsetto that reverberated across the phone lines, part of his persona, Kane knew.

"Turn the air conditioning up and keep the door closed. It'll only be an hour or so. Just make sure you're there to go through the motions with the detective."

Kane suppressed the receiver for a beat, dialed Bayonne's pager, entered a code number they had agreed upon, hung up the phone, and walked to the end of the bar.

Tae took a piece of paper from inside his topcoat and slid it across to Bruno. "That's the price I'm willing to pay per bar."

"That's twice what they're worth. Maybe three times in the case of Red Rum." Bruno scratched his chin. "You want to buy all three bars?"

"If you're comfortable with us moving into The Hill, we'd like to buy your properties on that side of the river. We don't want any hard feelings."

Bruno squinted at Tae. "I'll have to think this over."

Tae locked eyes with Kane. "Bruno, did you know Kane and I went to St. Catherine's together?"

"I think he mentioned it," Bruno said. "As I recall, I was surprised a zipperhead went to St. Catherine's."

Tae smiled. "Save the Seoul first, the boy second."

Bruno might not have heard the joke. Kane knew it was one of Tae's favorites.

"Kane, do you remember that story we read about how to kill an elephant?"

"By Eric Blair."

"George Orwell."

"How do you kill the elephant in the room?"

"You shoot it through the ear."

"That seems like something I'd remember."

Bruno drained his drink and set the glass on the table

hard enough to stop the conversation. "What are you two talking about?"

Tae Yoon Lee had the same high-pitched laugh he'd had when he and Kane had played basketball together at St. Catherine's. "Did Kane ever tell you how he got that scar?"

"He had an accident when he was a kid," Bruno said.

"We called it the devil's kiss, because it looks like the lipstick mark left by lips turned on their side."

"Why the devil's?" Bruno asked.

"Because if you knew Kane, the devil is the only one who'd get close enough to kiss his cheek."

"We were kids," Kane said. "We had lively imaginations." Kane took a rag from beneath the bar and scrubbed the counter, doing his best to avoid Bruno's eyes.

Tae said, "I'll tell you how he got the scar."

Kane said, "There's nothing to tell."

Bruno started to speak, but Tae cut him off. "Kane's first few months at St. Cat's were tough. The older kids wanted to teach a big kid like Kane a lesson. He was from the south side, and they didn't want him to gain a foothold. There were three of them, all seniors when Kane and I were sophomores. They picked on me, on Kane, anybody they thought was a threat. They'd shove our heads in toilets or beat us and shove us into lockers or garbage cans, wherever we'd fit. Kane fought back harder than the rest of us. He broke a guy's nose. The next week, they came into his room in the middle of the night, held him down, and held a red-hot blade to his face. They branded him."

Kane felt Bruno staring at the side of his face, examining

the scar to see if his skin had been seared by a pocketknife in the hands of three kids not old enough to vote.

"A lot of kids would've cracked then. They would've given up. Not Kane. Two weeks later, the weakest kid, the follower of that pack of seniors, got expelled. Father Ian, the principal, found gay porn in the kid's locker. The Benedictines are probably still enjoying that porn today. The poor kid was in St. Catherine's on a plea bargain. By getting expelled, he'd violated the terms of his probation. He was sent home, where his father beat him. He turned eighteen and spent a year in prison where everyone knew he'd been kicked out of St. Cat's for gay pornography."

Tae drained half his Guinness. He watched Bruno with his slanted eyes. "A month after that kid got expelled, the second kid, a football star and the muscle of the group, fell off the roof and broke both his legs. That bastard had been offered full scholarships to three different Division One schools. Now he'd never walk right again. He never explained what really happened, either, why he'd been on the roof of the dormitory in the middle of the night. He just said it was an accident."

"Tae," Kane said, "nobody wants to hear this."

"Bruno seems interested."

Bruno kept his mouth shut.

"The teachers knew these kids were a group, and they were starting to wonder why strange things had happened to two of them in such a short time, but why would they connect the two incidents? The only connection was that they were friends, and at St. Cat's, the faculty left well enough alone. Then the leader of the group disappeared."

"Disappeared?" Bruno asked. "What do you mean disappeared?"

"One morning, he didn't show up to class. One of the monks went to his room, and his bed hadn't been slept in. They couldn't find him."

"What happened to him?"

"They found his body a couple weeks later, duct taped, naked, inside a mausoleum in Lincoln Cemetery. If a groundskeeper hadn't noticed the door had been pried open, they might never have found the body."

"I heard about that, the kid from The Heights they found there. They thought it took him three days to die."

"Nobody fucked with Kane Kulpa after that."

"I had nothing to do with any of that. Nobody ever even suspected me. The kid had been selling dope in school, and he must've gotten on the wrong side of the wrong people. That's what everybody thought at the time. We were kids, and a few guys who picked on us came across some bad luck."

Bruno said, "Being buried alive is a bit more than bad luck."

"What would you do to someone who burned your face?" Tae shrugged. "Anyway, only three people know whether Kane was or wasn't involved, and Kane is one of them."

"How's that?" Bruno asked.

Tae drained the last of his beer. "Only two other people were there, two people Kane trusted, two people who'd been through similar things. Kane had friends back then.

He stood up for them, and they stood by him."

Kane nodded.

"Sometimes I wonder what happened to those friends," Tae said. "Sometimes I wonder what happened to friendship. I guess things change as we get older. Prison changes us. Tough choices might change us. Maybe we can't hold our ground forever. Everybody has to compromise sometime."

Bruno cleared his throat.

Tae pointed at Bruno while looking at Kane. "Maybe if we kept our friends close, we'd stay out of trouble."

Kane reached for Tae's glass, but the Korean motioned he was done.

Bruno said, "Why did you tell me this?"

"You're not a bad guy, Bruno. You should know by now how things are shaping up, and I figured you should know who you're working with. We all only get so many opportunities to act. You get me?"

Bruno stared at Tae's nose but didn't respond.

"Devil's kiss." Tae laughed. "Maybe the glory days weren't so glorious. Still, I'd watch out for this guy, Bruno. There's more to him than meets the eye."

Tae shook Bruno's hand. "You think about whatever you need to think about, but don't take too long. I look forward to hearing from you."

The door closed behind Tae, and Kane looked over the bar while he waited for Bruno to formulate and share his thoughts.

The bar smelled of stale beer and smoke. The ceiling was

stained a dark brown and leaked when it rained. A couple of windows had cracked or shattered over the years and been left the way they were or boarded up. Most of the stools and chairs sat unevenly, and the tables were cracked and chipped. Kane had spoken to Bruno about fixing the place up, but Bruno had always said that the place had character. Kane wondered if, all things considered, the bar gave the most efficacious impression.

"Jesus Christ," Bruno said. "How close were you two?"

"We were close. He was one of the few friends I had."

"What happened?"

"We graduated. I went to prison. He went to work with Tran."

"You haven't spoken since?"

Kane shrugged.

"I'm up against the wall, and you're buddies with the guy who's got me there."

"What did Tae want?"

"You know as well as anyone Tran Van Kahn's expanding. This was a follow-up to our conversation the other night."

"He wants to buy your bars on The Hill and offered to pay twice what they were worth? Are you going to sell?"

"I don't want to, but I don't know what else to do. I didn't want to come on too strong or come off too weak."

"Sounds pretty weak."

"Petey has gotten old, and I'm not the person who can replace him. I can keep the business side, but I'm not ruthless. I never was."

"That's not a bad thing."

"Sounds like you'd know."

"Tae exaggerated."

"Maybe so. In any case, action has been all fucked up since these killings, and now we've got another one. The cops have barricaded the front door, and Tran is kicking in the back."

"Which are you more worried about?"

"Tran is an animal, and he's moving fast. These bars are just across the river, but he'll get a toehold in St. Patrick's soon enough, whether I sell to him or somebody else does because that somebody doesn't want to make the decision to pay to us or pay to Tran. Selling out avoids being caught in the middle of a war."

"Was Petey much better than Tran back in the day?"

"Maybe not, but it felt like he was. I don't know. Tran's something else."

The phone rang, and Kane reached over and pulled the receiver form the cradle. "Bruno's."

On the other end of the line, Detective Bayonne said, "Kane, I got your message. I need you to come down to the precinct. Something came up."

NINE

———

MORE QUESTIONS THAN ANSWERS

6:28PM Thursday, September 3, 1992

Bayonne watched Kane's Buick Regal pull into the parking lot, flicked his cigarette into the bushes, and pushed off the wall to catch Kane before he went inside. Bayonne wasn't too worried, but he wanted things to run smoothly.

When Bayonne called his name, Kane turned on his heel, a quick, off-balanced motion.

"You a little jumpy today?"

"It's been one of those weeks. Why'd you call me in?"

"The precinct got a call about a man looking for girls. The caller described your Buick and the scar on your face. Dispatch was going to put out the description as part of the murder investigation, but the desk sergeant recognized it and passed it by me first. I told him I'd handle it."

Kane ran a hand through his hair and exhaled slowly.

"Thanks. You did me a favor."

"Do you know what this is about?"

"I might."

Bayonne waited for him to go on. When he didn't, Bayonne said, "You going to tell me?"

"Tran's making his move."

"What kind of move?"

"He's moved into The Hill, and he's making a play for the old neighborhoods. He's testing the water to see what Pete and Bruno will do."

"What are they going to do?"

"We'll see."

"Jesus." Bayonne's mind drifted to the violence he'd seen when Tran consolidated Waite Park. He shook his head. "Jesus."

"This might be a ploy by Tran to find out who my contacts are. If it is, you still want to parade me through the precinct?"

Bayonne shrugged. "It's too late to keep it a secret. We might as well go through the motions."

Bayonne turned to the row of black-and-whites, the beautiful cruisers washed and polished to a high shine. The precinct had seen better days, the brick was stained by the elements, and the roof had lost a few tiles over the years. When it rained hard, the detectives had to turn their trash cans into buckets to staunch the flood. But the patrol cars provided a row of order on the perimeter. Cleaned and refueled after every shift, they passed through the city like a silent reminder of what a policeman could be: bright, hard, visible, stoic, and beautiful. Central City Police Department, the words embossed above a silhouette of the skyline, and below, Protect and Serve.

Bayonne took the tin out of his back pocket and flicked it between his thumb and forefinger. "How serious is this?"

"I'd say the milk is way past the expiration date."

"I guess we shouldn't drink it." Bayonne shoved a wad into his lip. "Look. I'm going to let my new partner run the interview, okay? He's new and needs the practice. I'd rather he goes through the motions with you than somebody who's up against the wall."

"And it'll give you some distance. Sounds good to me. Did you take care of the other thing?"

"We've got a couple of black-and-whites, the ME and a forensic team at The Spanish Fly as we speak. My partner and I will head over after the interview."

They walked through the entryway, past the reception desk behind bulletproof glass, and Bayonne punched his code into the keypad. The lock clicked, and he escorted Kane past the desks and cubicles of the officers and detectives on duty. Nobody looked their way, but everybody watched.

Kane paused a moment in the door of the interview room and stared at Adam. He turned to Bayonne, raised an eyebrow, and turned back to Adam. "What the hell is this?"

Adam stood and opened his mouth to speak, but when he looked Kane full in the face, no sound escaped his lips.

Kane turned to Bayonne. "Vinnie, do you know what this is about?"

Bayonne raised an eyebrow and gestured toward a chair. "It's like I said, we just want to clear a couple things up so we can follow more reliable leads."

Kane said, "Adam is your partner?"

"Kane Kulpa?" Adam said. "You changed your name?"

Bayonne realized he'd missed something, and he had the feeling it was important. "Do you two know one another?"

Kane said, "Kulpa was Mom's maiden name. The church made me change it. They didn't want me to be known for a cop's death. Father Nick didn't want my past to haunt me. Turns out, that wasn't up to him."

"They said you were dead. I thought you died that night."

"I thought the same about you. You were in bad shape."

"Where'd you get the scar?"

"I've lived a full life."

Bayonne lifted the Pistons cap off his head and scratched his hairline. His gaze bounced between the cop and the criminal. The policeman, platinum blond, blue eyes, short, and round, almost the complete opposite of the streetwise bartender, tall, solid, with black hair and olive eyes. "Are you two related?"

Kane lowered himself into the chair that sat alone on one side of the table. "Adam is my little brother."

A few beats passed, and no one spoke. Adam took his seat across from Kane and put his hand on his open notepad. He cleared his throat and reached over to push the red button on the tape deck. "Mr. Kulpa, I'm Detective Adam McKenna. Please state your name for the record."

Kane told Adam he was a bartender at Bruno's, a bar

in Commerce City. He explained where he'd been on the nights in question, at the bar until one or two, and then home. He gave the names of a half dozen people who could place him at the bar for either or both nights. Adam scribbled in his notebook and fumbled through his paperwork.

Bayonne hadn't known what to say, so he'd let things run their course. He watched Adam and Kane go through the motions, neither looking at the other. He spit into a Styrofoam cup and scratched his beard. "Guys, this is weird. Why don't we turn off the tape and talk this through?"

Adam said, "Mr. Kulpa, we received a report that you were trolling for a specific woman, a prostitute. Is that true?"

"Yes."

Adam looked up. "You admit to soliciting a prostitute?"

"No. I was looking for the sister of a woman I know. I was trying to help her."

Adam returned to his notes. "How were you trying to help?"

"I wanted to get her off the street, to get her in a place where she could be supervised."

"Do you know why anyone would call in your description?"

"No. The mother of the girl I helped was placed in a rehabilitation program for confidential informants. The girl would've been without supervision. I thought enrolling her at St. Catherine's was the decent thing to do, her mother helping out and all. All of this is a matter of record."

Adam scribbled in his notebook. "Do you know the name of the supervising detective who had her admitted."

Bayonne caught Kane's look. "Write down the girl's name, and we can look that up later."

Adam slid the notebook across the table to Kane.

Bayonne reached across and clicked off the tape. "What the hell is going on between you two?"

Adam pointed at Kane. "He's a son of a bitch."

"What does that make you?" Kane said. "It's good to see you, too."

"I spent ten months in the hospital. Did you know that? Do you know what my foster homes were like? You didn't even try to find me."

"I thought you were dead."

"There were times I wished I was."

"I'm sorry about what happened."

Adam stood and crossed his arms over his chest. "You should be. It was your fault."

"It wasn't—" Kane shook his head, stood, and turned to the door. "Am I free to go?"

Bayonne glanced at his partner and raised an eyebrow. Adam shook his head and turned away from his partner only to face the scene's reflection in the mirrored glass of the observation room.

"Sure," Bayonne said. "I'll walk you out."

Before he left, Kane turned to his brother. "I'm sorry for what happened, Adam. I wish things had been different."

Adam placed his palm on the mirror, covering the place where his face had been reflected, the place, from his perspective, where he'd last seen his brother.

Once the door to the precinct closed behind Bayonne,

he grabbed Kane by the arm. "What the hell just happened in there?"

"Your new partner is my little brother, and we all just found out. That, and Tran sent me a message."

"Tran knows Adam is your brother?"

Kane shook his head, paused, then shrugged. "I doubt it, and you need to keep that out of any paper work. Destroy any tapes and burn any notes that might put me and Adam in that room. Find out if anyone was in the observation room if you can. Say I was questioned, and it didn't go anywhere. If Tran knows about Adam, he'll find a way to make sure I know. If he doesn't, we need to keep it to ourselves or it might put your partner in a bind."

"I'll do my best, but you know this place leaks like a sieve."

"I mean it," Kane said. "You need to personally destroy any record of this interview. Throwing something in the trash isn't enough."

Bayonne shook two smokes out of his pack and handed Kane one, then lit them both. They stood for a minute in the middle of the parking lot and sucked on their nails.

"Vinnie, you need to watch out for yourself, too."

"Me? When did I get enemies?"

"When you became my friend."

Bayonne stared at his cigarette, already half smoked. Nothing good ever lasted as long as you hoped. "Are you okay with this?"

"With what?"

"Me working with your brother?"

"I'm fine with it. Or I'll adjust. Whichever. I haven't seen him in a long time. He was eleven the last time. I hardly knew him. He's spent more years on his own than he spent with me and our father. He never really knew our mother."

"What happened between you two?"

Kane swallowed. "You know what? Don't worry about it."

Kane started walking, and Bayonne trailed behind, wondering if they had more to say. Kane turned to Bayonne and said, "Thanks for taking care of things at The Spanish Fly."

TEN

―――

HAVING THE CAKE YOU EAT

7:21PM Thursday, September 3, 1992

Kane backed into a parking spot in front of The Whistling Dixie. He could see Seth inside, watching Kane's Buick from a red plastic booth. Kane stepped out of his car, nodded to Seth, walked to the front door, greeted the hostess, and waved to one of the line cooks, who raised a metal spatula in Kane's direction as he passed.

The Whistling Dixie was on Arapahoe between 30th and Division Street, only a couple of blocks from Kane's house, and he'd been going there since before the original owner, Dixie Whistler, passed away. She and her husband had opened the place in the late 'fifties, and the combination of good service and cheap food had weathered the bear and bull markets. These days, the place was a bit rundown. The coffee mugs were chipped, the booths cracked, and the laminated menus bent. Children had drawn on many of the tables, and another coat of polish would do little to hide the cracks, scrapes, and divots in the linoleum floor.

The new owner, a sandy-haired, husky high school dropout who'd been hired as a line cook when he was seventeen, worked his way up to kitchen manager, and bought the place from Dixie's kids, had his work cut out for him. He stood, coffee pot in hand, discussing with Seth how far the Central City Spirits would go this season.

"If they can just stay healthy, they'll make a playoff run."

"Between the Pistons and the Bulls, I do not think they will crack the top of the central division. You kidding me?"

"Can I fill up your mug, Kane?"

"Sure thing, Dwayne. How's business?"

"Steady as always. You fellas give me a heads up if you decide to order anything. Otherwise, I'll leave you alone."

Dwayne was smarter than the stained t-shirt, complete with a picture of a steaming coffee mug behind a stack of pancakes, made him look. He was kind, generous, confidential, and gave Kane a wide, respectful berth.

Seth shook a packet of sugar before emptying it into his coffee.

"How was your interview?"

Kane didn't know how to answer that one. He told Seth about the anonymous tips giving his description, and he told Seth about Tae, one of their best friends from high school, being in Bruno's today. Kane left out the part about his brother, whom he hadn't seen in fifteen years, being a police detective.

"You have had one hell of a day."

"You don't know the half of it."

"Do you think Tran had the calls put in? How would he know you were looking for Crystal?"

"Who at The Saddle knew about it?"

Seth drank some coffee. "I do not know. Diamond and Amber. You think one of those two talked to someone?"

Kane stared out the window at the rear bumper of his car. "It's possible I was followed. Either of those two could've been talking about it in the dressing room or even with one of the johns. My guess is The Saddle has more holes than the clients can plug. In any case, it doesn't matter. This wasn't an important piece of information. Tran wanted me to know I'm being watched, and he knows I'm soft. Message received."

"I do not think you are soft."

"Tran's got us boxed in, and I haven't done a thing about it. That's soft."

"Are you going to do something about it?"

"Bruno won't. He doesn't have the fight in him, and he thinks Pete's over the hill, too."

"He is scared. That is smart."

"Tran has a reputation."

"Maybe you need to build a reputation for yourself."

"Tae was telling Bruno about how I got my scar, about what happened to those kids at St. Catherine's. He made it sound like I was someone to look out for."

"That is one hell of a story. Do you think it was a message, too?"

"Tran's not going to wait. If Bruno and Pete don't do something, there won't be anything left to do. Now's the time, and it's like they don't see it or don't care."

"If you are not scared of Tran, Kane, you should be."

"I wouldn't say I'm not scared. I just don't see the purpose of backing down. When Bruno was young, he had as much fight as anybody. Now he's got a wife, a nice home, and a batch of kids. He's got a lot to lose. I don't have that much to lose. I'd lose more by backing down."

"Are you trying to tell me you are not afraid to die?"

"I'm not saying that. I'm saying I'm more afraid of losing myself. I've seen what that can do to a person. The wrong kind of compromise creates the walking dead."

They sat in silence for a few moments, and Seth signaled Dwayne. Once they'd placed their order and Dwayne had taken their menus, Seth lit a cigarette and slid the ashtray in front of him.

"The girls talk about Tran, about his clubs and what it is like working for him. The stories are not pretty."

Kane had heard a few of the stories. Everybody had.

"Tran runs a lot of massage parlors and nightclubs. They say a lot of his girls are brought in through the docks in California. They are working off the cost of their passage, but he charges them room and board. By the time they are paid up, they are worked out and broken down. They might be forty or fifty years old, often sick, and they have no opportunity to raise a family and build a life. He is running a scam, a form of slavery."

"The wrong kind of compromises."

"You can say that again. He specializes in the wrong kind. They say he has got a place called The Dungeon, a place where he sells handicapped girls, girls with only one arm or only one leg or no legs, some weird shit."

Kane reached over and took a cigarette out of Seth's pack. Seth lit it for him. Kane wasn't much of a smoker, but sometimes he needed a boost.

"Amber said she heard that Molly Matches used to work there. She said that Matches worked there before she went back into rehab the final time. Amber said that most people do not know about it."

Kane locked eyes with Seth. "Where did she hear that?"

"I know you like Molly and everything. You feel sorry for her, but you know that she was on the sledge."

Kane felt sick and stumped out the cigarette. "Do you think Amber knows what she's talking about?"

"It is hard to say. Amber is as full of shit as anyone, but it does make sense. Where else is a girl like Molly Matches going to work? She cannot talk, and she was sick and strung out by the time she kicked. Who knows what skeletons dance in her closet?"

Kane couldn't argue with that.

"I am only telling you this so that you know what type of person Tran is. He is the opposite of you. You take Molly in and give her a straight job. He turns Molly into the worst version of herself. I think that Tran is the devil, or as close as we have in Central City."

"We're not complete opposites, Tran and me. We run

in the same circles."

Seth stubbed out his cigarette and leaned across the table. His hair looked freshly buzzed, and his muscles bulged beneath his pink silk shirt. "I believe Tran is the man who had my father killed."

"Wasn't your father killed in a car accident?"

"I do not know for sure, but Tran took over my father's club after my father died. This was back in the 'seventies, in Waite Park shortly after Tran came to town. He offered to buy the club, and my father turned him down."

"You want me to put up a fight so you can get revenge?"

"I want you to know that if you choose to fight, I will give it everything I have."

"I never doubted that."

"Why don't you buy Bruno out?" Seth asked. "You could take over his place and move into his position. He could retire, spend time with the family, and get a little kickback for the name. You practically run things for him anyway."

"Bruno still does a lot. I'm not even sure how many irons he has in the fire and how much is up to Petey V. Bruno might not have as much fight in him as he did twenty years ago, but I think Pete does."

"That is what I am saying. You and Pete could hold things down."

"I don't know. I've always gotten the feeling Bruno kept Pete sane. You know what I mean? Bruno is like Pete's conscience. I'm not sure I'd want to mess up the balance. Besides, Pete doesn't trust me like Bruno does."

"You cannot work for Tran. Between Pete and Bruno,

there is something human. They would never run a place like The Dungeon. They would not do things like Tran, and neither would you, shit like killing a man to take his business. They make money off the vices of people, sure. Bruno pays for his house with the paychecks of guys who work all day for the escapes Bruno sells them at night and on the weekends. But Tran, he sells something else. He sells the need and not the escape. He pushes people past where they want to go, and then he sells them the demons he put on their backs."

"You sure he's that different from guys like us?"

"I am sure. Abso-fucking-lutely sure."

Seth motioned that Dwayne was on his way over. He smiled and set a tall stack of pancakes in front of Seth and an egg white omelet with a side of fruit in front of Kane. He asked if they needed anything else, and they thanked him, no.

"How can you eat like that?"

"I love pancakes, so simple and yet so complete. Life would not be worth living without such treats. I do not eat them three times a day. I would not eat them three times a week. I never miss a workout, and I do not have to chase the ladies. You know they chase me. But, now and again, I indulge to my limit, and that is how I like to live. You, on the other hand, I am surprised you never became a priest with your restrictions, none of this and none of that. Those Benedictines at St. Catherine's must have gotten into your head."

He waved a forkful of pancake, syrup dripping to his

plate, toward Kane's face. "You should smile more. Things are never as bad as they seem."

Kane's pager beeped. He didn't want to talk about how often he smiled, so he excused himself and walked to the payphone between the bathrooms, in the hallway off the entrance. The call had come from St. Catherine's. Kane dialed the number and spoke to the school secretary. When Kane returned to the table, Seth had carved up his stack of pancakes and was drowning them in syrup.

"That was St. Catherine's. Crystal's gone. She didn't last a day."

ELEVEN

DARK DEPTHS
7:47PM Thursday, September 3, 1992

Andrews was a tall drink of iced tea served with a slice of lemon, hair so yellow Bayonne assumed it had been dyed, and at least one of his parents had been from somewhere warm. Between the hair and the complexion, Andrews could've been thirty or sixty. When he spoke, his words dribbled with a lisp and his hands explored the space between him and his audience, just a touch of jazz fingers.

"Welcome, Officers. It's always exciting to see men in uniform."

"We're not wearing uniforms," Adam said.

"Would you like to show me your badges?"

Bayonne held his ID in front of the man's face and exchanged a look with one of the patrolmen who had been holding down the fort. The patrolman grinned and looked away. Two squad cars were parked out front, and the medical examiner was done and waiting to remove the body. Bayonne asked Andrews to show him the body. They left the waiting room, two couches and three chairs in front of a check-in counter, and walked through a steel door and down a long corridor lined with small rooms each containing a massage table.

Andrews maintained a steady stream of banter in his flouncing castrato. "You can never be too careful, not with people being snuffed out left and right."

"It's easy to feel insecure with such a strong police presence."

"I find it invigorating, but I always like to know with whom I'm speaking, Detectives Bayonne and McKenna. I like to know who's who and which side of the fence they're on."

"Which side of the fence are we on now?"

"You may not play for my team, but you wouldn't be here if you didn't straddle the fence."

The man had brains. Bayonne asked him, as politely as possible, to tell them what had happened.

"We enjoyed the handsome devil's company two or three times a week. He always requested Sheila, whom he had known for some time, though on occasion he required the attention of a second young lady. Today, he seemed a bit tired, perhaps overwhelmed and already high. He came over with a group from The Side Saddle, three or four girls and a couple marks. The girls bring johns back and forth, coming here when they need a break from dancing or an empty room and going there when they need a drink or want to work the crowd. When business is slow, they roam in packs.

"Sheila scooped him up and carried him away from the other girls. She stepped out after the massage, giving the poor soul time to relax. I believe she felt he was taking a nap, and he'd paid for the time, in any case. Men seldom require the time they expect, no matter how enthusiastic or hopeful they may be. Sheila brought him a glass of water and chatted with the girls out front until we got a little busy. No rest for the wicked, as they say. Customers came and went, the nature of the business, such that Sheila and I hardly thought about the poor man. We didn't need the room at first, so I didn't worry, but another group came over from The Saddle. Three hours had passed, and Sheila knocked softly. When he didn't answer, Sheila opened the door and found him like this. What a shame."

Andrews gestured toward the room where two forensic technicians and the ME waited. Bayonne walked past them without acknowledging their impatience. The victim stared at Bayonne's shoes from the fetal position, his belt wrapped around his neck.

"Damn."

"Surely, Mr. Peters wasn't a friend of yours."

Bayonne crouched down next to Bernie Peters but didn't see anything that stood out. His body had been pulled off the table to be posed, but his clothes had been stacked neatly in a pile on a chair in the corner. While Bayonne questioned Andrews, he checked the evidence bags, nothing but a wallet, keys, gum, cigarettes, lighter, and condoms.

"How well did you know Bernie?"

Andrews tried to read Bayonne's face and then Adam's. The conversation had changed when Bayonne recognized the victim.

"Like I said, he came in two or three times a week."

"Did you see him outside of The Spanish Fly?"

"You mean socially?"

"I mean in an alley or on the street, sitting down, or on two feet, in a house or in a car, in your dreams wherever you are. Answer the damn questions, Andrews, or I'm going to process you for everything from pandering to solicitation to indecency. I'm sick of the funny business."

His face turned a lighter shade of butternut, and he motioned for the two detectives to follow him into the room across the hall. Bayonne told the forensic techs and ME they were good to go. Across the hall, Andrews closed the door behind them. Bayonne knew the room was soundproof, and he figured only a couple of the rooms had cameras, probably not this one.

"I never hung out with him," Andrews said. His lisp was gone, and his voice had dropped two octaves. "He wasn't my type, but he and Sheila were friends. They hung out a lot."

"What was he like?"

"Bernie? He was nice to me, but I think he just wanted to be welcome here. I don't think he liked me."

"You're a nice guy," Adam said. "Why wouldn't he like you?"

"He preferred the company of men who liked women, men like him. He was a hound. I hate to speak ill of the dead, but he was the worst type of man."

"Give it to us as straight as you can." Bayonne adjusted his Pistons cap. "That's not what I meant. Why did you think he was a bad guy?"

"He used people for his own satisfaction. Sex isn't that big of a deal. I know that, and if I didn't, I couldn't work this job. In order to work your job and deal with the type of people you deal with, I'm sure you know it, too. Intimacy is a big deal, though. Intimacy makes the sex worthwhile. Intimacy makes or breaks a relationship. Bernie didn't know intimacy existed. He used people to gain sexual gratification. These girls were tools for his masturbation. He needed the high sex brought him. Sex, drugs, alcohol, whatever he could get his hands on. The man was a degenerate, and most of the girls who sell themselves are lonely, even if they don't realize it. Bernie intuitively preyed on that. Sheila isn't and wasn't smart enough to figure that out. She's a nice girl, but Bernie Peters had her wrapped around his finger."

Adam said, "He wasn't that good-looking of a guy."

"With his kind of money, there's always an appeal."

"That's a fact," Bayonne said. "When did Bernie start using smack?"

"A few months ago. He was beginning to spiral, like his kind always do."

Bayonne nodded. "Where's Sheila?"

The interview ended, and his persona returned. "She's

down the hall with two of your beautiful boys in blue."
He saw Adam's eyebrows rise. "Dear me, only the officers
are on the clock. Who could enjoy themselves at a time
like this?"

Bayonne started for the door, paused, and turned back
to Andrews. "What's with the act?"

"You don't like the show?"

"It's not that." Bayonne lifted his Pistons cap and ran a
hand through his hair. "It's your business. Don't worry
about it."

Andrews chuckled. "Our clients don't like competition.
Most guys who come in here want to believe they're special. They want to feel a connection. The girl may work for
a living, but with him, she's different. She feels something.
We're selling a fantasy. If I make a show of it, I don't come
off as a fly in the Vaseline."

Bayonne said, "You've got this thing figured out,
don't you?"

***

Sheila sat between the two uniforms, her eyes on one
and her left hand on the forearm of the other. Petite in an
almost childlike way despite being in her mid-twenties,
she wore a black tank top and blue jeans, and she flicked
her cigarette toward an overflowing ashtray. Her bottle-blond locks had chestnut roots, and she had a crooked
nose with a protuberance of bone in the middle, a prominent piece of her face's asymmetry. Her makeup looked
good, especially for a woman who'd worked all day.

"You can't blame yourself," one of the officers said.

"These things happen. You never can tell what the day might bring."

"We take that to heart in our line of work," the other officer said.

The two cops had both seen the backside of their forties, and one, Bayonne knew, had a daughter who'd recently graduated from college. Yet both were caught in Sheila's spell, a sexual blend of vulnerability and assertiveness, need and defenselessness, awakened desire and inexperience. Watching her for a few beats, Bayonne doubted she knew what she was doing, which made him wonder where the instinct came from.

"I know you're right. There's just so much violence these days. First Mikey and now Bernie. It's getting so a girl doesn't feel safe going to work."

Bayonne coughed in the doorway. The two officers smiled and sidled past him, disappearing down the hall. Bayonne began with the basics. She told the same story Andrews did, and although she knew Jimmy Mason, had known Mike Connolly, and had, she claimed, at times, hung out at Mason's and at Alfie's, she hadn't been at either place when the murders were committed.

"How long had you known Bernie Peters?"

As she had felt, instinctively, that her appeal would work on the officers, after a minute with Adam and Bayonne, she knew it wouldn't work on them. She sat up, put both feet flat on the floor, rubbed her nose, and lit a new cigarette.

"He'd been coming here for three years, but I met him

before that. At a party downtown."

"What kind of party?"

"It was for someone in the mayor's office, I think. There were a lot of politicians and rich people there. I went with some other girls, and me and Bernie hit it off. He started coming here after that."

"You've worked here for three years?"

"Closer to five."

A couple of scars were visible in the creases of her elbows, healed track marks, but nothing recent.

"How long have you been clean?"

"Almost a year."

"Did Bernie help or hinder?"

"What?"

"Did Bernie use?"

"Bernie had gotten a little wilder lately."

"What do you mean? How had Bernie changed since you first met him?"

"When we met, he'd never been below Riverwalk Drive."

"Did you introduce him to the party scene down here? Introduce him to some of your friends, hook-ups and the like?"

"Everybody needs a friend, and Bernie had a lot of money. He was a good guy. We had a lot of fun together."

"You said he'd gotten a little wilder?"

"When we met, he'd put anything up his nose, and he popped, but he wouldn't use a needle. Something changed a few months ago. He started spending more time in Waite Park. He seemed high when he came in today, maybe a bit higher than usual. I'm not sure what all he was into anymore."

"To each his own."

"That's my philosophy."

"Was he into anything strange? Strangulation? Anything like that?"

"You mean the belt? No. That wasn't us. He never did anything like that with me."

"Did he ever get physical?"

"Maybe a little sometimes. A lot of guys are into that."

"Did he like to give or receive?"

"He tried it both ways."

"Most guys go one way or the other."

"He was more of a giver."

"Had he gotten more physical lately?"

Sheila nodded.

Bayonne paused for a minute trying to think of another question, some way to mine the connection he'd discovered between Bernie's life uptown, his shift toward slumming, and his growing predilections. Bayonne just didn't see the connection to the murders. He looked at his partner, and Adam shrugged. Bernie was no longer a suspect.

Sheila touched Bayonne's arm. "Bernie wasn't a bad guy. He was one of the good ones. He loved a good time. He might've gotten rough lately, but he didn't want to hurt anybody. He was just trying to have fun. He was safer than most of the guys I meet."

"How rough did he get?"

She looked away. "Rough, sometimes."

Bayonne couldn't think of anything else to ask her, so he thanked her and gave her his card.

TWELVE

BLOODY REFLECTION

Noonish, Friday, September 4, 1992

Shortly before noon, Bruno walked into the bar that bore his name. He was wearing a gray-and-yellow flannel shirt, blue jeans, brown loafers, and a Stetson cap. Kane, who was cleaning behind the bar, reached for the stereo and turned down the volume on Sam Cooke, great music to begin the day. Bruno put his cap on the bar and bellied up, and Kane placed a gin and tonic, Bruno's usual morning medication, within reach. Bruno stared into the drink and mumbled along with the music. He pointed at the stereo and asked Kane to turn it back up before draining his drink in one draw.

Bruno pulled a soft pack of Winston lights from the pocket of his flannel and flicked one into his hand. As he lit the nail, Kane put an ashtray next to the empty glass.

"Gino, my oldest, he got into Loyola. You believe that?"

"He going to play ball there?"

"If he doesn't, they won't pay his tuition."

"Good for him. Good for you, too, Bruno."

"I needed some good news."

Bruno slid the highball glass in Kane's direction, and Kane refilled it for him.

"Did you talk to Pete?"

"I met with him last night, and he's going to think on it. A couple guys paid to Tran this week. This has been a long time coming."

"If guys are already paying to Tran and Pete has to think, the time has passed."

"You might be right."

"You need to decide what you're going to do."

"Do you think we have a choice?"

"There's always a choice."

Kane drank his coffee, and Bruno drank his gin and tonic while Sam Cooke faded, and the CD changer, on random, slipped to the Reverend Al Green.

Kane said, "Have you ever heard of a place called The Dungeon?"

"I've seen it with my own eyes. That's not a place you ever want to go."

Kane pulled the coffee pot from the maker and refilled his mug. "Why not? What goes on there?"

"The Dungeon is a place that caters to men who want to lose their souls. The whole idea of the place is to take away any rules or sense of right and wrong. In a place like that, you can do whatever you want. Nobody should be able to do whatever he wants. There's gotta be some point where enough is enough."

Bruno took a long drag on his smoke and exhaled slowly. "Guys go there because they want a taste of power. They want to know what it feels like to control someone. But they can't stop. They have to go back again and again. You don't ever want to open that door. You don't want to know what lies inside other men's lives. Or what's inside you. Freedom can be a horrible thing."

No wonder he went to church three times a week. "You know the janitor at The Side Saddle?" Kane asked.

"Molly Matches?"

"Did she ever work there?"

"Maybe. She's the type of girl who'd find herself there, a girl who can't talk, might be a little slow or just off. Years ago, she went on the skids. I used to see her on the street, trying to turn a trick, looking like she hadn't washed in days. She was in a bad way."

"Did you ever try to help her?"

"She wasn't my problem. She never worked for me." He took a drink. "What difference does it make? Some people you can't help. You can't fill the hole inside them." Bruno finished his second drink, slid the glass toward Kane, and sucked on his cigarette. "Why are you asking me about this shit? I've got serious things to deal with."

"I'm trying to get a sense of Tran."

"Well, you've put your finger on it there. Tran is the type of guy who takes advantage of those who can't help themselves and uses them to twist the souls of those who should know better. He put more than a few people in his pocket because he caught them on video at The Dungeon. He'll do anything he can to get one over, get a leg up. He's a ruthless bastard."

Kane placed a new drink in front of Bruno, and they both stared at it for a beat.

"You're saying Tran's a bully."

"We're a ways from the schoolyard, kid."

"How do you plan to handle this bully?"

"If Pete bodies up, I'll back him. If Pete rolls over, I'm going to retire. I'll sell to Pete or Tae or Tran or whoever they want, and I'm going to go watch my youngest play ball and spend my days with my grandkids and my wife. We'll have loud family dinners every night, and I'll get just drunk enough in the afternoons."

"You're a little young to retire."

"I don't feel it." Bruno yawned. "What do you want me to do? You look like you've got some fight in you."

Kane leaned back and thought this over. "I've never thought of myself as a fighter."

"You don't know what to think of yourself." Bruno's giggles sounded like a drowning Muppet. "I knew that the second day in jail. You had no idea how to carry yourself, how other people saw you. You try to out-think your problems when a heavy hand would push them aside."

"I've never thought of myself as some great thinker."

"But it's the strength you rely on most. You're always

contemplating, considering, seeing things from every angle. You've been behind this bar for how long? Five years? You've worked for me longer than six. You should've been out on your own a couple years ago. Pete would've backed you. You know I would've. But what do you do? You bide your time and buy your buildings and a couple of bars. You're spinning your web. That's what my wife says. She thinks you're a spider."

"I'm not trying to catch flies. I'm just trying to keep from being a fly in someone else's web."

"If you were the man Tae said you were, Tran wouldn't have us against the wall. You were the future, Kane. Pete and I have been waiting for you to take the reins."

"What the fuck do you want from me?"

"I want the kid who fights back, the kid who breaks noses and throws people off roofs."

"I was never that person, not really."

"I think you are. I think you always were. I think, deep down, you're a ruthless, heartless son of a bitch, and it scares the shit out of you."

Kane raised an eyebrow at all that.

"Kid, nothing scares you more than how little you feel for the pain of others. I wish to god I had that problem."

Bruno had exhausted the conversation, so they sat in silence a few ticks. Kane stared at the bar, and Bruno stared into his drink.

"Did I ever tell you about the time Petey put a bullet through a kid's stuffed animal?"

"I think I'd remember that one."

Bruno wiped at his eyes, sipped his drink, and spoke with his hands. "This was back 'fifty-eight or 'fifty-nine, when we all wore leather jackets and used pomade. We were still working out of Pete's mom's place. She worked the laundry over at St. Luke's, and we'd just started moving enough to get noticed. We were sitting in Pete's mom's living room, weighing and bagging, and listening to her forty-fives, something by Dean Martin. Pete was singing along with that sweet tenor of his. I never could carry a tune. Anyway, I thought I heard something, so I looked around. Something hit the far wall, a few feet above the record player. Pete must've heard it, too. He stood, walked over to the record player, and lifted the needle. This time we heard the shot, a real light pop, and a bullet hit the wall about two inches from Pete's face. He turned and walked to the window, leaning over the back of the couch, to see a guy hanging out of a Cadillac, aiming a little twenty-two in his direction."

Bruno had to pause to catch his breath. He'd been overcome by another case of the giggles, and the CD changer flipped discs to play "Walk Like a Man," by The Four Seasons.

"Pete's mom's house was on Twenty-third and Jefferson, elevated up on that slope toward the river like those houses there, so the knuckleheads had to shoot up at an angle. The picture window was double-paned, a storm window, so by the time the little twenty-two bullet made it through both panes, it had nothing left. It bounced off the plaster on the far wall." Bruno gave Kane's forearm a squeeze.

"Pete didn't know that. All he saw was two guys he knew, in a Cadillac he recognized, shooting up his mom's house and almost shooting him in the face.

"Petey grabs his thirty-eight off the coffee table and runs out the front door, down the front steps to the street, and up the sidewalk, gun blazing. He shoots out their back window, blows out one taillight, puts a hole in a mailbox, and one bullet, a stray, knocks the cotton bunny out of the hands of a four-year-old girl playing in the yard across the street.

"The Cadillac disappears around the corner, and Pete is standing there staring at the girl. The girl's staring back at him. She's never seen a gun before, and the stuffed animal is sprawled on his back, stuffing floating in the air and flaking the lawn. Pete shoves his pistol in the back of his pants, walks over to the girl, kneels down, and starts giving Bugs Bunny mouth-to-mouth. He tells the girl he's gonna be fine. He turns to me and tells me to get some bandages from under the sink. When I get back there, he grabs some gauze, tapes the bunny up, and gives her this bandaged toy, saying he's good as new. The girl just stares at him.

"The next night, Pete stops by the neighbor's house and gives the dad a new stuffed bunny. He'd gone all over town to find a replacement that matched the bunny he'd shot. The dad was angry at first, tried to give Pete a piece of his mind. Pete just put his hand on the guy's shoulder and said he didn't have to replace the bunny. He didn't have to do anything at all, but he wanted to make things right as best he could, and there wouldn't be any more trouble around that little girl. We moved into The Taproom a week later, and Pete's been working out of there ever since."

"The guy was okay with that?"

"I think he moved his family up to The Hill or Uptown a year later, something like that. I don't know which."

"What happened to the two guys in the Cadillac?"

"They wound up in the lake, and Elmore Washington took over things in Echo. His nephews still run things there. Can you imagine Petey running down the sidewalk, shooting at a car in the middle of the day?"

"I can't imagine anybody doing that."

"That's what it means to body up. The fight has to come first, before the people you love and before the random guy or kid on the street. Still, like I said, you have to have limits. People who destroy just to destroy, who enjoy it." Bruno shook his head. "I could never understand that."

"How long has it been since there's been bad blood?"

"About fifteen years. Maybe less."

Kane refilled Bruno's glass, and Bruno took a small sip, slowing down now that the first three drinks had leveled him off.

"Everything was changing in the late 'seventies, and there was a lot of money to be made, more than ever before. It took a few years to figure out the balance. There'd been a lot of people coming over from Asia because of all the nonsense with communism and playing dominos. Waite Park was barely a neighborhood back then, and houses started popping up in clusters around shopping centers. Koreans, Vietnamese, and Hmong started to carve out their space, and other people tried to stop them.

"We'd always been friendly with Elmore and his people in Echo. We respected each other's boundaries, but Elmore got into it with one group of Koreans, some refugees. We split a few hairs with your people in St. Patrick's. Once Tran came out ahead in Waite Park, the noise died down. Everybody figured out their place, and, for the most part, we've had peace since."

The CD changer hit a scratch and began to skip.

"Things were different then," he continued. "Now, everybody's used to peace. The cops, the people who spend their money at our bars and with our girls, they don't want a fight. Fights cost too much."

The front door opened, and a man, silhouetted by the sun at his back, raised a pistol. Bruno turned toward him and froze with a confused look on his face. He should've seen it coming. The man fired five shots, four into Bruno's chest and one into the wall behind. Bruno's body jumped like a marionette. The man turned toward Kane and paused when Kane, too, froze. Kane had a look on his face every bit as stupid as Bruno's. The man flicked the barrel of the gun, giving Kane a second to get out of the way. Kane ducked, and the man emptied the pistol into the mirror behind the bar. Shards rained on Kane's head, cutting his cheek and hands.

When Kane heard the door slam shut, he waited a few ticks on his hands and knees and cast a dirty look skyward, toward the powers above. He blinked several times, stared at the tile near his face, and wondered why his mind didn't work. He slowly stood and looked at the fragments of the mirror that still hung to the wall. In his shattered reflection, he saw himself streaked in blood, Bruno's blood that had sprayed across him, and the blood dripping from his face, arms, and hands. Pulling a piece of glass from the side of his palm, Kane heard a cough.

Kane hopped over the bar and checked on Bruno, staring at the ceiling and trying to catch a steady breath. He still had a faint heartbeat, but there was nothing to do. Kane reached behind the bar, pulled the phone off the hook, and punched nine-one-one with a clean knuckle. Kane held Bruno's head and put pressure on his chest while Bruno gurgled away the final moments of his existence.

THIRTEEN

A DRINK BEFORE
7:04PM Friday, September 4, 1992

Bayonne took his new partner to Book 'Em's because it was a Friday night and their investigation had stalled. Book 'Em's, obviously a cop bar, was conveniently located across the street from St. Patrick's precinct, sandwiched between a bail bonds office and a pawnshop. In the long, thin, watering hole with a proper bar along one wall and a row of booths along the other, they sat in the booth farthest from the street and the light of day. Above their heads hung photographs, images of famous Irish Americans like the Kennedy brothers, Gene Kelly, John Huston, Donald O'Connor, Raymond Chandler, and Jimmy Braddock. The white, green, and orange hung on the back wall above the jukebox playing John Feeney singing a Caoineadh. Bayonne wasn't Irish, so some of the faux nationalism felt like malarkey, but Book 'Em's was his precinct bar, and the jukebox also played Sinatra, Dino, Elvis, The Righteous Brothers, and a wide selection of jazz.

A pack of Camels, two whiskeys straight, and two pints of Guinness sat between Bayonne and Adam, and the kid had been holding his own for the hour they'd been there.

"So, just to recap," Adam said. "Our only legitimate suspect turned up murdered. His widow has an airtight alibi, and we've got no other real leads."

"Yes."

"We've identified the two John Does, an unmarried insurance salesman from Uptown and a divorced electronics repairman. Neither had any enemies or close relatives, and their apartments and work gave us nothing."

"Right."

"They were both regulars at The Side Saddle, Spanish Fly, and Alfie's, but there is no other connection between them and Michael Connolly, Art Spencer, or Bernie Peters."

"Correct."

"We've got no theories and no suspects."

"That sums up the situation."

"What do we do next?"

"You're looking at it."

"We're just going to drink?"

This kid had a lot to learn. "The weekend started. There's nothing we can do to hurry things along. We're running background checks on the girls at The Saddle and Spanish Fly, and we've sent out feelers among our informants, but until we get something, we've got no way to narrow our list of suspects. Sometimes, you just have to take a deep breath and let your subconscious do the heavy lifting. Lighten the load, as they say."

Adam sipped his Guinness, and Bayonne lit another cigarette.

"What are your hobbies? What do you do to pass the time, unwind after a hard day?"

"I don't know. I have a Super Nintendo and a Mac Two-e."

"I don't know what that means."

"I like computers and video games."

"I'm sure that's a great way to meet people. Me, I like to read about history. Can't get enough of it."

"I thought you liked to watch basketball."

"That, too, but the Pistons might've peaked, and even after living here more than twenty years, I can't get myself to watch The Spirits. In any case, I've been reading a lot of history."

"Does it bring back memories?"

"It helps clear some cobwebs."

They chuckled at that, and Bayonne took a drink.

"I tried to read about Vietnam, but the historians get it all wrong. They have the facts right, but they don't realize what it was like. They always focus on a gimmick: the troops' drug use, American imperialism, the subjugation of this group or that. They tell stories to sell books, but they don't care about the truth."

"You know the truth?"

"I doubt it, but I was there. As I recall, it felt more sobering and more confusing than anything I've ever read."

"My dad was in the war."

"Oh, yeah? What branch?"

"He was a Navy helicopter pilot. He helped evacuate the wounded, I think."

"I didn't know that. It was a hell of a job. I worked as a medic. I might've helped load guys onto your dad's chopper."

"Maybe so."

Bayonne knew Adam's father had died years ago, and he didn't know where to take the conversation, so the two men sat with their thoughts for a few beats and struggled with the implications.

Adam said, "How well do you know Kane?"

"Nobody knows Kane, not that well."

"But he's one of your CIs, isn't he?"

Bayonne glanced around the bar, but nobody was close enough to be listening. "What do *you* know about your brother?"

"I hadn't seen him in fifteen years until the other day. I didn't know he was still alive."

"And you haven't heard anything? Now that you know his name, you haven't asked around?"

"I asked my old training officer, and he said Kane works for Bruno Pantagglia, but he didn't really know what he does. He acted like I should leave it alone."

"I don't know what he does either, to be honest, but yeah, he's a CI. He gets me information and I kick him a few bucks now and again. Sometimes, when it's necessary, I keep storms from brewing as long as I don't have to break the law. He's the reason we got the case."

"You don't break, just bend the law."

"That's how it works."

"You kick him a few bucks, and he kicks back to you."

"If I didn't take a taste, I wouldn't be trusted. We all get something, you know that."

"Did you really bust him, years ago, like you said?"

Bayonne nodded. "He was twenty-one the night he got arrested. He'd been drinking with a few friends, and they went ditch-diving along the highway west of the city. They were in a Bronco, sliding along the snow in the ditch and pulling back onto the road. I'm sure it was a lot of fun until they hit a tree, got stuck, and by the time they got back on the road, a good Samaritan had called the cops. They were pulled over when they hit the city limits, lights flashing in front and behind. The guy driving made a run for it. I guess he knew there was three ounces of pot under the backseat. Kane slid behind the wheel and put the vehicle in gear, but the muzzles of three thirty-eights stopped him cold. The two guys in back walked, and the driver got away."

"Jesus. You pulled him over?"

"Nope. I was working narcotics back then, and the two kids in the backseat I suspected of dealing but had nothing on. On the basis of that bust, I got warrants for everyone in the car and searched their apartments. I came up with nothing on the two kids in the backseat, but I found three more pounds of bud and an ounce of yeyo in the ceiling tiles of Kane's apartment. Your brother spent three years in prison."

"You sent him up?"

"I did, and I'd never heard his name before the night he was in that car. Nobody had. I also watched him during the trial. He wasn't a bad kid. He was three months from graduating from college with a dual major in philosophy and history. I probably ruined his life."

Bayonne took a sip of his whiskey to make what he was about to say easier. "I looked into your brother's history a little, pulled a few strings and got a glance at his juvvie record. I learned about his time at St. Catherine's, the correctional institute for troubled teens run by Benedictines. That's a tough place for anybody, but he managed to get a small academic scholarship to Central City State University. He was slinging dope just to pay his bills and keep himself in school. He still got good grades and maintained his scholarship."

"How'd you two get connected?"

"After he got out, I looked him up, offered to help him get a job. When he took the job working for Bruno, he got back to me, offered me information if things were getting out of hand."

"That simple?"

"I warned him that Bruno's bar was a drop, but he said he could take care of himself. I figured he was right. Bruno's not a bad guy and neither is your brother. People are just people. Most things are that simple."

Maybe the kid didn't know what to say to that. In any case, he didn't say anything. He swallowed half his whiskey and chased it with a gulp of beer. Adam and Bayonne sat in the dark booth, listening to "So What" off *Kind of Blue*.

A thread hung loose from the conversation. Bayonne tugged on the thread and felt a few ideas shift into place. He opened his mouth and described his thoughts as best he could. "My wife was Vietnamese. She was seventeen when we came to her village. I was nineteen."

Adam sat back in his seat, so Bayonne kept talking. "We set up a field office in her village. She was beautiful, and innocent. Her parents hated me. They were killed in a Vietcong night raid. Who knows which side got them? I think that question lingered in the back of my wife's mind. I know it lingered in the back of mine. I married her because I loved her and because I felt bad. I didn't want her to become a prostitute. I didn't think she'd been one, but times were tough in those villages. Their farms became defensive perimeters, and their shops became supply dumps. We fought in their backyard, and when we got there, the enemy followed. The people had no way of making a living. It was like we didn't go to war; we brought the war with us. Anyway, I wanted her to have something to live on, and a married soldier made more, so . . . . Well, we got married."

Bayonne took a sip of whiskey and lit another cigarette. "I did three tours over there, met her on the first tour, married her on the second, and brought her home after the third. We hardly knew each other. I'd spent more time on patrol or on leave than I had in her village, but I'd supported her, and, in a way, she'd supported me. I don't know who felt a greater debt to the other, but I think that was our connection, indebtedness and guilt. I didn't want to bring her back to Detroit, and I had nothing to say to my parents, so we came here. I went to work for the department, and she stayed home. Her English got pretty good, and she took a job in a bookstore she liked to go to. It was owned by an old guy from China who'd taught biology at the university."

Bayonne stopped talking because he didn't know what to say.

"What does she do now?" Adam asked.

"She died. We separated, and she moved into an apartment above the book shop. There was a fire. The book store burned down."

"My god."

"The same guy owned half the block. The property was worth more than the building, and it was easier to burn it down for insurance than to tear it down and rebuild. Nobody knew she was living there. It wasn't a proper apartment, just a room with a bathroom."

"I'm sorry, Vince."

"Yeah, well, I don't think I ever knew her all that well. After it happened, you know, things didn't really change for me. She'd been gone a long time. We'd just never filed for divorce."

"Still. . . ."

"Anyway, my point was, that's how things work. Nobody could prove arson, and nobody wanted to. The wheels were greased, and my wife was buried. I learned a hard lesson, that family is important, but you need to work at it. You can't take it for granted."

Miles Davis faded away, and the jukebox clicked and clacked over to the King asking if anybody was lonesome that night.

"I think something's going on between Tran Van Kahn and the guys Kane works for."

"What are you telling me?"

"I'm saying your brother might be in some trouble."

"He's made his choices."

"Some of those choices were made for him."

Bayonne's memory strained to a bright sunny day when he kissed his wife and called her sweetheart. For a moment, his heart filled with pain and he wished she'd come back again, even if only so he could learn, truly and deeply, how insurmountable their differences had been. Since none of that was going to happen, he finished his whiskey, motioned to the bartender for another round, and lit a new cigarette off the butt of the old.

"You know," Bayonne said, "the answer is usually something simple."

Adam looked up from the spot on the table he'd been studying. "What?"

"The case. The john killer. The killer is usually the person who was there and had the most to gain. Our job is never as hard as we think it is."

"Now you tell me."

"Why would I lead with a disclaimer?" Bayonne flicked his cigarette toward the ashtray. "Is there something obvious we're missing?"

"How drunk are you?"

"Watch yourself, kid. I'm probably soberer than you are. Soberer? More sober? Soberer, I think. Anyway, what I'm saying is, if we're missing something obvious, there's a reason. If we move that reason out of our way, we'll see the obvious answer."

"How do we find the reason?"

"We look at our assumptions. What do we really know?"

"Fuck all?"

Bayonne asked, "How did this start?"

"The insurance salesman."

"And we don't know where the electronics repairman died."

"Couldn't you make a call?"

"Nobody's going to talk about this shit. They want this thing to go away."

"We know he was a regular down here."

"All the victims except the electronics repairman were connected to Alfie's."

"Okay."

"The repairman was a john, too. Some lonesome asshole trying to find a good time. There but for the grace of God . . . ."

Adam said, "You believe that? You think we're all the same? You don't think these guys were pathetic?"

"Maybe, but for the grace of God and a few dozen self-destructive choices." Bayonne took a long drink. "I've seen people I thought were standup guys crumble beneath the weight of desires they didn't even know they had. I've seen drugs twist people into pieces, and I've seen people sell their bodies and degrade themselves without realizing how far things had gone. People struggle. It's what we do. Do you really think you're better?"

"Yes. At least I try to be. I certainly don't pity these guys for getting caught with their pants down and straps around their arms."

"You make a good point."

"What happened to all your sympathy and understanding?"

Bayonne waved his cigarette toward Adam like he was warding off his negativity. "Not your judging. That's not a good point. That's just you being a dick. I meant about the guys being the same. Everybody but Connolly was from the other side of the river. Waite Park, Uptown, and The Heights are a long way from St. Patrick's and Commerce City, and even Connolly was a slave to his desires. They were easy targets."

"They were outsiders, off the rails or tourists, and weak by south side standards."

They thought on it a moment.

Adam said, "You think everybody was killed for the same reason?"

"That's simple enough, isn't it?"

"Maybe. Maybe it's too simple. Why were they posed?"

"I don't know, but maybe we should check out The Side Saddle. These guys were regulars there, and we never talked to the janitor."

"You said she was handicapped."

"She's a bit of a retard, but we need to check her off the list. Besides, we're drinking here. We might as well drink there and see what we see. If this guy is picking off the weakest members of the herd, we might be able to see what he sees, pick up his trail."

"You want to question someone after you've been drinking?"

"She's a retard. We're just following up on one last thing. Let's get a glass of water and wait an hour. We'll be fine."

FOURTEEN

TIES THAT BIND
6:52PM Friday, September 4, 1992

More than six hours had passed since Bruno had been killed. Kane had given a statement to the cops and been sent on his way. Two old bulls had been given the case, guys leaning toward retirement who could be cut loose if needed. Kane knew what would happen next. Until everyone had a sense of which way the ball would bounce, the investigation would stall, and the papers would relegate the shooting to a middle page. Bruno's killer would never be arrested, but the case would be brought to resolution once the best outcome could be agreed upon.

The way of the world.

Molly was working, so Kane had the apartment to himself. He'd taken a shower, put a Donald Byrd album in the CD player, and decided to try to read, get his mind off things, when he heard the knock. He closed the doors to the bedrooms and checked to make sure nothing of Molly's stood out before he worked the chain.

Tae Yoon Lee greeted Kane with a smile.

Kane said, "Of all the gin joints in all the world . . . ."

"I'm here on some difficult business. You mind if I come in?"

Kane stepped aside. "It seems difficult business is your bread and butter these days."

"Don't I know it."

Tae had changed a lot since they were kids. He looked pale, and he'd lost weight.

"Tran wants to talk to you. Petey V was shot and killed in his car outside of his office this morning, less than an hour after Bruno."

"You've been busy."

"You know I don't like Tran any more than you do. Less."

"You've worked for him a long time. It makes it hard to trust you."

"Glad to hear it. That will make what I'm here to say that much easier."

"What are you here to say?"

"We're past the point of no return. Your options are Tran's way or the highway."

"We knew it would come to this. Let's not act surprised."

"Then what are you upset about?"

"I watched a friend die today."

A few beats passed as the two men thought about what to say.

"You want a beer?"

"Sure." Tae sat on Kane's couch and crossed his legs.

Kane opened two Newcastles and put one in front of Tae, and asked, "How do you think the Irish and Italians started working together?"

"They went to church together."

"Half the Koreans I know are Catholic, including you. Pete and Bruno consolidated the old neighborhoods around the time Tran took over Waite Park. The Irish lost that fight."

"Look at you now."

"That's what I'm saying. These situations have a life of their own. We need to take a beat."

"We don't have time to wait and think. That got Pete and Bruno killed."

"You killed Bruno."

Tae shrugged. "Tran's message is that you work for him now. I feel as though I've conveyed the gist of that."

"Do you have any more news?"

"Waite Park, Long Beach, The Hill, and Uptown pay to Tran already. With Petey V and Bruno gone, there's no opposition south of Riverwalk. That leaves just the Jackson brothers in Echo, Barry Lynch in Midtown, and Tricky Rickett in the downtown fifteenth ward. Lynch and Rickett will cater to Tran in the hopes he won't muscle them out."

"What was all that shit you told Bruno about my scar?"

"I gave Bruno every opportunity. I thought that would make you feel better, and I never had anything against the guy. If you wanted to save Bruno, you should've done something."

"You could've been more direct."

"What the fuck are you talking about? Did you want me to draw him a fucking map? Tran laid it out for you at The Taproom. I expected to hear from you after that."

"I've been dealing with some shit, and I didn't know if we were on the same page, working toward the same goals."

"Are you going to blame me for doing what needed to be done? You didn't react, and the wheels kept turning. Tran has momentum. We need to move hard and fast. Tran's not somebody you want to fuck with. If he can use you to his advantage, he will. If he can't, he'll dispose of you. He won't hesitate for a second, and he's the best chess player I've ever seen. Better than you."

Kane noticed one of Molly's sweatshirts hanging over the back of a chair.

Tae said, "We've all made our choices, even if you chose not to make a decision."

Kane considered that for a few ticks. "What's he got on you? Why are you working for a guy like Tran? I never asked because I thought it was your business, but now I want to know."

"A lot's changed since we knew each other."

Kane sipped his beer.

Tae looked at the closed bedroom doors. "Anybody in there? Anybody listening?"

"Nobody in here but us chickens."

Tae ignored the reference, or didn't get it, and his response surprised Kane. "You stood up for me at St. Cat's. I still owe you for that, and I want to make good on that debt, so you listen to what I'm saying. I went to work for Tran after school. I was picking stuff up and dropping stuff off, nothing serious. I rode along on a couple of things. At first Tran seemed like a good enough guy. I knew what type of business I was in. Anyway, what was I supposed to do, take a job in a factory? Push a pen my whole life? I was a poor chink with a juvenile record and an average transcript from St. Catherine's. I didn't have that many options.

"Then I saw what Tran was really like. He made me watch while he tortured a woman in front of her kids. Two kids, maybe twelve and ten, and he broke the woman's fingers until she agreed to sell him the laundry business her mother had started. It had been in the family for thirty years, and Tran wanted to redevelop the land. There's an apartment building on the property now, some shithole with a view of the mall." Tae swallowed hard. "A few weeks later I tried to quit, and Tran put me off, told me to think about it. I was afraid, but every few weeks I mentioned making a change. He asked me to go for a ride with him. He said he'd expected something like this might happen. He drove me down to the massage parlor where the woman worked. She wasn't giving any massages. The fingers on her right hand pointed in six different directions. In a little over five months she'd gone from owning a family business to selling herself. What was a single mother with a high school diploma and a bad hand going to do? Tran had broken her."

"Damn."

"That's not the half of it. He showed me where she'd be in a year, a place called The Dungeon. You heard of this place?"

"Yes."

"You ever been there?"

"No."

"You don't want to see it, Kane. You don't ever want to go there. There isn't enough booze to wipe the memory of it away. That place is the reason society has rules."

"What do you mean?"

"You can do whatever you want there. The mice are at the end of their ropes and dancing. City councilmen and district attorneys go there. Tran watches the high-end clients at The Dragon's Mane. He waits for their appetites to grow, and when he thinks they're ready, he introduces them, little by little, to a wider array of vices. Tran has them hooked on the power, the ability to force someone weaker to do their bidding, to do horrible, degrading things. Tran gives his clients a taste of true control, and once they've felt it, truly felt it, they can't get enough."

"That's enough to hook people?"

"Probably not, but it's enough to tempt them. Tran records them. He gets evidence, audio and video."

"He blackmails them."

"Not just blackmail. Tran knows that if you give a guy two options, one that allows him to do what he secretly wants but is ashamed of or feels guilty over, and the other option amounts to a public penance and sacrifice, paying for guilt and admitting to crime, a guy will keep sinning. Tran pushes people to lose control, to give in to their worst desires. That's his secret, his power. He knows what it means to give options that aren't real options."

"You kept working for him after that?"

"He told me that if I ever walked out on him, he'd kill my mother and my brother, and my sister would spend the rest of her short life working in The Dungeon." Tae shook a cigarette into his palm and stuck it between his lips. He was shaking so badly that he had to hold the zippo with both hands to light it. "You can't fight a man like that. No one can, not directly. He'll do whatever it takes to win, to control." Tae took a long drag on his cigarette and spoke into the exhale. "He's pure evil."

"Maybe he is."

"Now you know what you're dealing with in Tran Van Kahn. You know you only have one option."

"Do all of Tran's guys feel the same way you do?"

"Most do. A couple don't. The guys who like to hurt people, Tran lets them."

Kane thought about that a moment. "You know who is who?"

"I think so."

"What about Yung?"

"He's a good guy. Growing up with an uncle like that . . . . Yung's got his demons, but he's a decent guy."

"Is there a story there?"

"There's a lot to it, but the gist is that there's no guarantee that Yung inherits the kingdom. Tran keeps everybody off balance, especially blood."

"Family can be funny. They can hate and love the same relative."

"Yung never hurt anybody."

"Would he hurt his uncle if he could?"

"I don't know. I do know he's ambitious. If his uncle weren't in his way, he'd want a place at the trough."

"So, back to my question: Are we ready for this?"

"Are you? Nobody thinks you're a real player, Kane. You sit and watch but never get your hands dirty. We're going to need to get our hands dirty."

"Maybe we do."

"What changed? Your rage used to be closer to the surface. Something softened you. Maybe it was prison. I don't know, but you're behind a wall now."

That was true enough.

Tae said, "You have to go at Tran sideways. He fights dirty, so he can't know you're coming. Criminals these days are too honest. Everybody's worked together so long they don't know how to fight dirty."

"And if I still remember?"

"I'd say it's time to prove it."

"No time like the present."

The clock on the wall ticked toward the next hour, and Tae finished his beer, dropped the butt of his smoke into the bottle, and shook the remaining liquid to douse the cherry.

"You're here to take me for a ride, right?"

Tae nodded.

"Let me grab my things."

Kane stepped into his bedroom and, with his back to the open door, grabbed the keys off the top of his dresser and clipped a small Spyderco onto the sleeve of his thermal. He pulled a black hoody on over the thermal and adjusted the cuff. He pulled on his leather jacket back in the living room, and motioned toward the door.

Tae stopped him. "Whoever else lives here isn't a girl-friend. If this doesn't work out, Tran can never know about her. If Tran finds out you have family, he'll use it against you."

"I know that."

"Good."

"Is my secret safe with you?"

Tae nodded once, opened the door, and Kane followed him into the night.

FIFTEEN

SPIRITS ON OUR SHOULDERS
8:28PM Friday, September 4, 1992

The Side Saddle's red brick, windowless façade stood out among the concrete and glass storefronts of the more recent additions to the neighborhood's business district. The mason had left an inscription near the front steps, House of Perpetual Succor, 1883. Run by the O'Malley sisters, two lay ministers of charity, and receiving a small stipend from the church, the building had once been a boarding house for young women who came to the city looking for work, daughters of rural, Catholic families whose parents needed the extra income or simply couldn't afford another mouth to feed. Many of those women found corruption in the unforgiving streets. Many fell into the easiest profession available to the young, unskilled, attractive, and naïve. Others met men who said one thing and did another, men who left them vulnerable, broken, angry, and disabused of their innocence.

The O'Malley sisters died of dysentery in 1902, and three nuns took over the house, ruling it with a firmer grip than had been in the will or ability of the lay sisters. The church closed the house during the Depression, and the building eventually fell into disrepair.

Midcentury, it was reopened and remodeled as an apartment building, only to fall out of use again in the 'eighties. A couple of years ago, the deed was purchased by a holding company with a local address, and the building had been remodeled, walls torn down, a parquet dance floor instead of a dining room, a small stage beneath a slanting stairwell, thick red carpet, small tables seating three or four in place of the parlor, and a bar complete with a mirror, stools, and several coolers where once had been a kitchen. The place catered to fantasies, a high-end house that simultaneously serviced both the body and the imagination without descending into perverse proclivities.

When Adam and Bayonne walked into The Side Saddle, they weren't drunk, exactly, but they weren't sober, strictly speaking. They knew what they were about, or had convinced themselves they did. They'd grasped the loosest string in that knot of a case yet unraveled. In hindsight, they shouldn't have pulled so hard and should've had a better plan.

Bayonne and Adam were unprepared for what greeted them within that House of Perpetual Succor. If the Marquis de Sade's bastard daughter had gotten lost between a fantasy and a nightmare, she might've gotten directions to The Side Saddle. From the entryway, the two detectives faced their own distortion reflected in a tainted mirror behind the bar that extended the length of the far wall, ending at a hallway.

Seeing himself stretched and flattened, a blur of flesh that blended with the red of the carpet, the mahogany of the wall, the parquet, and the mixture of flesh provided by the denizens of the house, gave Bayonne a queasy sensation. Between the mirror and the bar, Karla, a buxom brunette in a skintight yellow dress, smiled. She turned to exchange pleasantries with the male bartender, a giant of a man, giving Bayonne a clear view of the angel's wings tattooed over her shoulder blades.

Bayonne saddled up to the bar and ordered a Jack and Coke from Seth. Adam fidgeted on the stool by Bayonne's side. The bartender set the drink in front of Bayonne and pointed a finger, the thumb cocked like a hammer, at Bayonne's partner.

Adam said, "Nothing for me, thanks."

The bartender said, "You sure? You know you are in a bar."

Bayonne's face swam in the bent looking glass behind the bartender. "Seth Gromski, I'd like you to meet my new partner, Adam McKenna."

The pollock extended a hand to Adam, and the young detective's fist disappeared inside the bartender's.

"It is nice to meet you. You gentlemen are not here about a case? Not on a Friday night."

"We wanted to speak with the janitor, Molly Matches," Adam said.

"If you do not mind my asking, have the two of you been drinking?"

Adam opened his mouth, but Bayonne beat him to the watering hole. "Not so much you'd notice."

"Did I not?"

Bayonne winked at the giant and leaned back. "Let's just say, we've only just noticed."

As sure as you're born, the big fella put three shot glasses on the bar and ran a bottle of Jameson over them. Normally Bayonne didn't like to mix his whiskies, but, you know, a gift horse and all that. The barman raised his glass, and the law met him in the middle.

"To solving crime," he said.

He removed the shot glasses, mixed himself a vodka tonic, and leaned on his elbows between the two detectives. Music erupted on the loudspeaker and the curtain opened on the stage.

An elastic young woman in a leotard swung a leg up on a pole and spun in a circle. Bayonne lit a cigarette. Adam stared open-mouthed.

An older woman, maybe mid-fifties, five-feet five-inches tall with larger than average breasts, short, curly blond hair, and buttermilk skin, pushed a mop bucket past the top of the stairs. She wore a blue bandana beneath her hairline, blue jeans, and a white t-shirt. She kind of looked like Rosie the Riveter, though if memory served Bayonne, Rosie never worked in a whorehouse.

Bayonne leaned across the bar and spoke to the bartender. "Is that Molly?"

"You are welcome to talk to her as long as you are gentle, but maybe you should wait until tomorrow. What do you think?"

Adam turned to the two, oblivious of the conversation, and ordered a beer. He'd been pulled into the scene by the persuasive powers of the contortionist's body language.

Adam asked, "Where did she learn to use her legs like that?"

"Some of us have natural talents."

The three of them laughed to hide their insecurities in the face of blinding, nubile femininity.

Karla caught Seth's eye, and Seth smiled and tapped the bar. "I will be right back."

Bayonne watched Seth lean into Karla, and the two of them whispered back and forth. Karla surveyed the room. It was early yet, and there were only a few men drinking and making time at the tables. Several employees sat by themselves, chatting and watching their colleague suspended from the pole, her bra hanging off one arm. Karla walked over to the table, said a few words, and two of the mice stood and walked toward the detectives.

Bayonne tried to move, but the girls were too quick.

One of the girls, a tall brunette with a high forehead and pale blue eyeshadow, sat next to Adam. The other, an older woman with a larger frame, sat next to Bayonne. Her muscles were well defined, not the type of woman you'd argue with if you didn't have to, which may have

202 | INDY PERRO

been the point.

Bayonne spoke to himself as much as to Adam or anyone else who might've been listening. "When we've finished these drinks, we'll need to speak with Miss Matches."

The woman near his elbow smiled. "Whatever you say, Officer."

Bayonne nodded for effect, then he felt a hand on his leg.

"What kind of gun are you packing, Detective?"

The detectives had no intention of being rude, so they chatted with the ladies for a few minutes. The dancer on stage completed her set, and someone new replaced her. Bayonne bought the escorts drinks, which meant he had rocks in his head. Maybe forty-five minutes passed before Molly walked down the stairs and into the hallway near the bathrooms and office. Bayonne watched as she used a key to unlock a utility closet.

Adam leaned over to his partner. "Is that Molly Matches?"

"Yeah. We should talk to her when we get a second."

"She looks familiar."

"What do you mean? Do you know her?"

"I don't think so. I don't know. There's something off. Maybe I've seen her before, somewhere."

"How could you forget a woman like that? Platinum-blond hair and almost identical skin?"

"Yeah. It's just...I don't know. I don't feel well."

"Take it easy. Maybe you need some air."

"I'll be all right."

The janitor walked by them with a tub full of cleaning supplies and ascended the stairs. Bayonne felt a hand on his chin, pulling him toward temptation.

Adam said, "I'm going to use the bathroom."

Bayonne waved a hand at his partner but didn't see him go up the stairs rather than down the hall to the restrooms. Seth nodded at the girl to follow him. The mouse next to Bayonne was telling him about the cosmetology degree she'd been pursuing for eight years, which was a surprisingly interesting story, in part because he thought she'd said cosmology. A few minutes passed before Bayonne realized his partner was gone.

"Where's Detective McKenna?"

Seth set a Jack and Coke in front of Bayonne and poured them each a shot. "Relax. He went upstairs."

They clinked glasses, and Bayonne swallowed the Jameson. "I better check on him."

The giant put a hand on Bayonne's wrist and shook his head. "Our girls do not go in for that sort of thing, unless you pay extra."

They heard a shout followed by a scream over the music, and something struck the floor above. Bayonne followed the big man up the stairs, his gun drawn.

They found Adam in a room with Molly Matches. He was shaking her by the shoulders, and she was squirming, trying to break free from his grasp. The girl who'd followed Adam was on the floor, leaning against the wall near the door, like she'd been pushed there. She was screaming obscenities at Adam.

"Why won't you speak to me?" Adam shouted. "What is wrong with you? Where have you been?"

Seth and Bayonne stood in the doorway for a second and watched the strange and confusing sight. A cop, a sheet, sheet and a half to the wind, shouting into the face of a brain-damaged mute he'd never met, asking again and again, louder and louder, why she won't talk to him and where she'd been. No one knew exactly what was happening, and no one was hurt.

The mute squirmed, and Adam yelled, as though screaming would repair her vocal cords. Awkward as it was, the scene certainly wasn't the strangest or most disruptive thing that had ever happened in The Side Saddle.

Seth helped the hooker off the floor and pushed her out the door. When he turned back to the room, he paused next to Bayonne. Bayonne took the opportunity to reflect on the fact that it had been several minutes since his last cigarette, and he could've used one in that moment.

Seth leaned toward Bayonne and spoke in an inside voice. "You take care of your partner, and I will help Molly."

Seth and Bayonne stepped forward, and Bayonne wrapped his partner in a bear hug, pinning his arms just below the shoulders. Seth pulled Molly out of Adam's clutches, and the poor woman lost her balance and plopped to the floor. She sobbed, sprawled on her back, her mouth opening and closing silently, guttural groans coming from deep within. She rolled onto all fours, blond hair disheveled, and opened her mouth, a lioness, queen of the jungle whose roar had been reduced to the wet smacking of her tongue against the roof of her mouth, or perhaps Rosie the Riveter, silenced, and forced onto her hands and knees.

Adam tried to push Bayonne away, and when the older detective wouldn't release the young man, Adam started to scream. Bayonne held Adam as tight as he could.

Seth pulled Molly from the floor and pushed her into the arms of one of the girls clustered in the hall to watch the commotion. He ushered everyone back to work, closed the door, and turned to face the law.

"What the hell just happened?"

Bayonne didn't know, so he spoke to the back of his partner's head. "What's going on here, buddy? What happened? What's wrong?"

"Let me go. I need to talk to her. Where's she been?"

Seth said, "That was Molly Matches, the janitor here. Who do you think you were talking to?"

When Adam didn't answer, Seth grabbed the young man by the front of his shirt and pulled him out of Bayonne's arms.

"What the hell is wrong with you? She cannot speak. She has not spoken in years. She is handicapped, not right in the head, and neither are you. You cannot treat her that way."

Bayonne put a hand on the man's shoulder. He wasn't wrong, but it was best if he didn't talk to a cop like that.

Adam said, "She's not a janitor, not in a place like this."

"She is," the Pollock said. "That is exactly who and what she is. What is your problem with that?"

Adam went limp in the big man's arms. The fight just went out of him, and the bartender, like so many bartenders before, said something to the defeated man that was both oddly true and yet utterly illogical.

"You and she are a lot alike. Neither of you make sense."

Seth released Adam onto the bed, and the young detective rolled over toward the wall and sobbed like a baby.

Seth ran a hand through his hair. "Sober up. Pull yourselves together. I need to make sure Molly is okay. You two stay in here until you get it together. I do not want you downstairs fucking up the action."

The giant disappeared into the bowels of lechery, and Bayonne turned to face the nightmare Seth left behind.

"That isn't Molly Matches," Adam said. "Her name is Molly McKenna."

SIXTEEN

DEVIL'S DUE

8:12PM Friday, September 4, 1992

Kane followed Tae up to Waite Park and left his Buick next to Tae's Honda in a lot behind The Dragon's Mane, the hottest nightclub in that part of the city. Tran Van Kahn held court in the basement, and the security kept out the tabloid journalists, gossip columnists, pickpockets, con-artists, and general degenerates. To get in, you had to be beautiful or know somebody or both. No fleas in The Dragon's Mane, only young professionals looking for a good time dancing the night away with local celebrities, politicians, millionaires, gangsters, and professional party girls. In the Dragon's Mane, if you could afford it, you could attain it, a saying they should've tattooed on their foreheads or at least stamped on the backs of their hands. It was a place to see and a place to be seen.

Kane had laughed the first time he'd heard the name:
The Dragon's Mane. Discotheques, with their sweaty
grinding, music too loud to hear yourself think, and over-
abundance of party drugs, held no draw for Kane. He figured they might as well have called the club The Donkey
No Go Dance Party, until he realized the place's potential.
Tran, by catering to his own security and privacy needs,
had created a haven for the city's elite, a clientele that now
felt comfortable approaching their host with personal
problems or desires. Over the years, sure enough, The
Dragon's Mane had become the heart of Tran's empire,
pumping blood into all his enterprises and nurturing the
growth of his extending limbs. They say the name rolls
off the tongue in Vietnamese and gets stuck in the ear, or
something like that. Maybe it did.

Kane followed Tae around front where they had to step
into the street to get around the corral of self-absorption,
a long line of young people lacking looks, prestige, money,
and generally too inadequate to enter. Tae nodded to a
man with a radio connected to his ear. The man pushed a
button on his waist and spoke into a microphone clipped
to his shirt. He waited a few ticks, acknowledged the voice
only he could hear, and opened the door for Kane and Tae.

Two bars, one lighted blue and one red, were on either
side of the door, which opened to a dance floor with sofas
and tables along the walls made of floor-to-ceiling mir-
rors, where the reflections of the gyrating mass flashed
to the visual beat of the strobes. Women in body paint
danced on platforms above the crowds, and in offbeat

darkness, their bodies glowed fluorescent.

Tae parted the sweating sea and, when he and Kane reached the far wall, Tae punched a seven-digit code into a keypad and a door with no handle clicked open. Kane followed Tae into the wall, down a hall of private rooms, some of which sounded as though the party had continued full swing, and down a flight of stairs. At the end of the underground hallway, Tae knocked on a door, which was opened, and Kane met Tran Van Kahn for the second time.

Tran and two goons stood in a room that looked like an oversized utility closet. A concrete floor sloped to a drainage grate, and the naked cinder blocks gave the walls an institutional, penal quality. A water heater, chest freezer, and sink lined one wall. The rest of the room was empty except for the folding chair in front of Tran.

Tae nodded to Tran and took his place to Tran's right, next to the two guys with shaved heads, only one of whom was big enough to frighten Kane.

"I'm glad your old friend persuaded you to pay me a visit."

"He's not my friend."

"I'd hoped we could all be friends here."

Tran wore his signature pin-striped black suit that set off his long white hair and beard, the dragon's mane. Tran played with his beard while he spoke. If it weren't for the bottomless pools of darkness that were his eyes, he looked like something from the mind of Jim Henson.

Tran motioned for his guest to take a seat, and since Kane didn't see a way to avoid it, he sat in the folding chair in the middle of the room, in front of Tran and in front of Tae and the two goons, all of whom, Kane knew, were carrying guns. The drainage grate below the chair didn't help put his mind at ease either.

"You're an easy man to recognize. Your scar marks you."

There wasn't a question there, so Kane didn't give an answer. The old man reached toward Kane. His fingers stopped an inch or two from Kane's face, and Kane could feel, or thought he could, a warmth emanating from Tran's fingers. Kane's scar itched, just a little, like a wound healing.

"Some say you were branded. Others say you were kissed by the devil. Most don't say anything about you. I must admit, from the right angle, your scar resembles the lips of a woman."

"The paled lipstick of a fading beauty. I get a lot of compliments."

Tran's eyes narrowed, and his fingers returned to his beard. "Mr. Kulpa, I have heard a lot about you. My nephew says you are a man to be wary of. Tae Yoon Lee, my associate, says prison changed you. He thinks you've gone soft. Which is it? What kind of man are you?"

"I'm not going to explain myself to you."

"I think, if nothing else, you are an intelligent man. I think you understand where you are. You understand you have only two options."

Kane understood that Tran saw only two options, but he didn't want to interrupt Tran's train of thought, so he said nothing.

"I hope that, no matter who you are or how you've changed, you are a man who understands his limitations and listens to reason. I know that you are an up-and-comer in your part of town. I would like you to take over the clubs and businesses of your former boss, Mr. Bruno Pantagglia, and several of the late Peter Di Vittorio's. You have lived beneath their shadows long enough. Now is your time to rule in the old neighborhoods. I have a list prepared here of the clubs in question. Would you care to do that?"

"I hadn't planned on it. I try to avoid too much responsibility."

"Unfortunately, Bruno and Peter are no longer with us. We do need to find a replacement."

"What makes you think I'm the man for the job?"

"My informants tell me that you have been running several of the clubs already, and you are familiar with the day-to-day operations of all of them. Therefore, your taking control would be a smooth transition, and we could all maximize our profits."

Kane turned his face away from Tran.

"My associate and your friend Mr. Tae Yoon Lee vouches for you as well. He believes you would be an excellent addition to our little family. You would, of course, be required to pay me forty percent of your illicit earnings."

Here, Kane thought, was his opportunity to stall, to gain a little breathing room. "Forty percent? You're joking. No one has ever asked for more than twenty. You'll be squeezing me dry."

"You're right that it hasn't been done, but this is a new day, Mr. Kulpa. Several members of your cohort are already paying me forty percent. They understood the nature of change. If you do not, someone else will."

"I don't know about any of this. I need—"

"You are in no position to argue, Mr. Kulpa. The time to fight has passed, and you know it. Your former employers could've mounted an opposition, but they did not. Neither did you. Everyone will pay to me. Everyone. Don't you understand that by now?" Tran stroked his beard.

"I thought there were boundaries, rules that kept any one person from getting too strong. I thought everyone respected those rules."

"There were, and they did. I do not. Times change. I am the embodiment of that change."

"I can't pay that much."

"I thought you might say that. I want you to understand that you have no other options."

Tran nodded to one of his men, the short guy next to Tae, and the little man walked to the door, opened it, and said something in a Sinitic language into the hall. Kane noted that although he was short, he wasn't a midget, exactly, not like Tran. In fact, Kane gained a whole new perspective on his size and strength when the man stepped behind Kane and placed his pistol against the back of Kane's head.

Two men dragged a naked female form into the room, laid her on the floor between Kane and Tran, and left, closing the door behind them. Crystal Molloy, her hands and feet tied with bailing twine and her eyes rolled back into her head, was sweating and mumbling against the piece of cloth in her mouth.

"Miss Molloy has been working in one of my clubs, a place called The Dungeon. Perhaps you've heard of it."

Kane tensed, and the guy behind him smacked him with the tip of his pistol.

"Do you know Miss Molloy, by chance?"

When Kane didn't respond, the guy behind him smacked him with the tip of his pistol again.

"I know you picked her up, got her into St. Catherine's, and put her mother in rehab, where she remains, by the way, until we decide to have her removed. We did, after all, remove Crystal here from St. Catherine's."

Tran knelt in front of Kane, though he didn't need to. Apparently, Tran wanted to look up into Kane's face.

"Nothing goes on in my city without my knowing. Nothing. I had to ask myself why a man like you would spend so much time on a slut like her. You know her, and she means something to you."

Tran stood, walked around Crystal's writhing body, and removed a small caliber revolver from inside his suit jacket. Tran walked back to Kane, smiled, and shot Crystal Molloy in the head.

Tae jumped.

Kane didn't blink.

Crystal's corpse twitched as the small caliber bullet ricocheted in her skull.

"If you don't work for me, I will kill the Polish bartender.

I will kill the busty Italian madam. I'll kill Bruno's wife, children, and grandchildren. I'll burn The Side Saddle to the ground. I'll kill that cop from Detroit you seem to like so much. You think I don't know about you? I know everything there is to know about you."

Tran had stopped stroking his beard. His chest rose and fell. He watched Kane, like a vulture watching a corpse he circles. A few ticks passed, and the only sound in the room was Tran's breathing.

Kane chuckled. "Are you ever going to get around to killing me?"

The man behind Kane cocked the pistol pressing into the base of Kane's skull.

Kane said, "All this time and the gun wasn't even cocked? And here I've been pitting out."

Tran made a motion with his hand, and the pistol came away from Kane's cerebellum.

"I will kill you last, Mr. Kulpa. Once you've watched everyone close to you die, I'll kill you slowly, with my own hands."

"All this for money?"

"Money? Don't you understand yet? This isn't for money. The money is nothing more than a means to an end. This is the end. This position I've put you in is the point. Didn't Pete and Bruno understand that? This is all about power. You'll do what I want you to do or you'll cease to exist. That's what this is all about. That's what everything is about."

"I don't think we're on the same page."

"There is only the one page."

"In fact, we're not reading the same book. We're not even in the same library. You don't know anything about me. I met Crystal for the first time two days ago. You mean more to me than she did, and you don't mean shit to me. Something would've gotten her eventually. If not today, tomorrow or the next day. If not you, someone like you. She meant nothing to me."

Kane decided it was time to have a difficult conversation, one he'd been putting off. He stood and began to pace the room, talking with his hands.

"I've known for months you were making moves. You're not as subtle as you think you are. Everyone's been watching you. You're a bull in a Vietnamese shop.

"I helped Crystal because it was the right thing to do, not because I thought I'd make a difference or make a friend or because I thought she was worth the effort. I helped her because she was a kid who needed help, and when I needed help, somebody helped me. That doesn't make me weak. It keeps me sane. That's something you'll never understand, Tran, and it's something you don't know about me because you can't understand it. As it happens, my heart doesn't bleed. I just don't believe in posturing or pushing people around to feel powerful."

Kane stopped with Tran on the other side of Crystal's body, and Tae behind Tran. Kane pointed a finger in Tran's face and tried to spray while he spoke, though his mouth was dry.

"You don't understand me," Kane said, "but now I understand you. I'm going to deny you the thing you want. Kill me or kill whoever you need to, but I'll never work for you. Never."

Tran stepped forward into the pool of Crystal's blood, and he and Kane were only a foot apart. Tran raised the small caliber pistol and pointed it at Kane's belly. Tran's eyes had a wildness to them, and his gun hand shook with rage.

"I'm going to kill you, but not yet. Not today. I'm going to make you watch—"

Tran was close enough that Kane could smell the cordite from Tae's pistol. The bullet went through the hinge of Tran's right jaw and up through his brain and lodged in the concrete ceiling, spraying dust. As Tran's body hit the floor, Tae stepped over Crystal and shot the short man in the face.

The other man in the room looked at the bloody white mane on the floor, looked up at Tae and Kane, looked down at his colleague's short corpse on the floor, and looked again at Tran's collapsed face, framed by the bloodied mane.

Kane broke the spell by clapping his hands. "What took you so long? I was running out of things to say."

"I got caught up in your speech about helping people. Moving stuff."

The other guy turned away and vomited in the corner. Tae put his gun in its holster, walked over to the guy, and patted him on the back. If he'd had any hair, Tae might've held it back. Tae said something in Vietnamese, and the man nodded, wiped his mouth with a handkerchief Kane hoped hadn't been used, and walked into the hall.

Tae motioned toward the guy he'd shot. "He was one of the men I told you about, a man loyal to Tran."

Two men entered, pushing a cart overflowing with rolls of colored plastic, rubber gloves, and cleaning supplies. One of the men handed Tae and Kane each a towel. They wiped away the evidence as best they could.

"I wore black for a reason," Kane said.

"I see that now."

They left the cleaning to the professionals, and Tae led Kane out the back door of the club.

Tae put a hand on Kane's arm when they were next to their cars. "Now it's done. What next?"

"I think this means you're the grand poohbah."

"Uneasy lies the head and all that." Tae lit a cigarette. "I'm not sure there can be a grand poohbah. Tran's days were numbered. If it hadn't been me, it would've been somebody."

"You think you just put a target on your back?"

"I opened a void. That's for sure." Tae shrugged. "I'll be fine if I step Tran's boys down and if you help me. You consolidate the south side. We talk to the Jacksons and back off the rest of the locals. Let everyone know Tran's gone. If everybody's making money again, everybody's happy. Things go back to the way they were."

"Sounds like Humpty Dumpty. Nobody on The Hill will trust The Pastor after this, and there're similar voids in The Heights and Midtown. Without Tran to keep the peace, there'll be a lot of local power struggles, and a lot of people have been bored for a long time. They've been craving the chance to grow their businesses."

"There'll be some of that, sure. That's why I need the old Kane again, the Kane who took care of those kids at Saint Cat's."

"What if that Kane no longer exists?"

"You're a cold-blooded son of a bitch, always were."

Kane stared up at the sky and Tae puffed on his nail. Two guys stumbled out of the back door of the club beneath the weight of something bulky and awkward rolled in opaque plastic. A few steps into the parking lot, they stopped while one of the guys held his end beneath one arm and fumbled in his pocket with his other hand. The plastic bundle slipped and hit the blacktop with a smack. The two men cussed at each other, and one turned a key in the trunk of a Ford Taurus. They tossed the load in the trunk. One of the guys said something and the other laughed. They walked back into the club.

"It's good to see people enjoying their work."

"I'll back your play, Tae, but don't expect too much out of me. I don't know that I can run things in the old neighborhoods. I've got obligations I need to see to. There are other things going on right now, and I need to tread carefully."

"What other things? Is that why you've been so distracted?"

Kane didn't know what to say to that, another conversation he didn't know how to have. "I don't want to become like . . . like Tran or . . . ."

"Violence was never your demon, Kane. Compassion was always your demon. You'd let people you care about destroy you, and you'd call it kindness. You think the fact that you don't feel what you think you should feel makes you a bad person. It doesn't. Tran was a bad person. Those bullies at Saint Cat's, at least the ring leader you buried alive, he was a bad person, a date rapist and sadist. You're not a bad person. You're a survivor. One day the people you care about will corrode you, and you'll only have yourself to blame."

"Is that why you waited until after Crystal was dead?"

"You should've known Tran had her. He had those tips called into your precinct. You knew he knew about her. Besides, I only had the one shot. I needed to come from behind. You said she didn't mean anything to you."

"Did you know he had her?"

"I didn't know who she was until a few minutes ago."

Kane didn't believe that. "She didn't deserve to die in a nightclub's basement, have her body dumped in the trunk of a Ford."

"Would you prefer a Chevrolet? She won't stay in the Ford long."

"What about Bruno? He had a wife and kids. Did you need to kill him?"

"Had Pete and Bruno acted, things would've gone differently, but they didn't. You knew Tran was coming. This whole thing was your plan. You asked me to put you in a room with him. You said it needed to happen on Tran's turf, with you as a hostage, and I needed to pull the trigger.

You wanted it to happen in a way that kept fingers from pointing. That set up never would've worked without Bruno dead. If you wanted to, you could've popped Tran on the street, done it yourself."

"That would've started a war. I explained that it had to be you."

"And Tran needed to overreach. All I'm saying is you knew it was coming. Bruno's time had come and gone. You knew he had to go."

"Meet the new boss. Same as the old boss."

Tae flicked his butt into the night and walked toward his new office. "What the fuck ever. You think about what you need to think about. Decide what you can and can't live with, but don't forget, I'm the best friend you have. We're in this together."

SEVENTEEN

LOVE, DEATH, AND FAMILY

9:37PM Friday, September 4, 1992

As Bayonne dragged a dazed Adam down the stairs in The Side Saddle, Kane walked in the front door. Kane saw the two detectives, froze, and looked at Karla behind the bar. Karla scowled. Kane, in charcoal Silver Tabs and a black hoodie beneath a black leather jacket, moved toward the two policemen.

"What are you two doing here?"

"Are you covered in blood?" Bayonne asked.

"It isn't mine. What happened? What's going on?"

Adam pushed Bayonne aside and jabbed a finger into Kane's chest. "You've had her here the whole time. You didn't tell me."

"Jesus Christ." Kane stepped back and put both his hands up in surrender. "I saw you yesterday for the first time in fifteen years. When would I have told you?"

"Goddamn you, Kane."

Kane slapped his brother across the face. It took Bayonne by surprise, both because people didn't usually strike police officers, even police who are a bit drunk, and because it was kind of a sissy thing to do.

Kane pushed his brother beyond the bar and into the hallway that led to the restrooms, supply closet, and office. Kane stepped in front and opened the door to a room with a couch along one wall that faced a desk. The wall across from the door had a sink and a mirror set in it, and a mobile bar had been pushed next to the sink.

"Take a seat. You, too, Vinnie."

Adam and Bayonne sat on the couch, the cleanliness of which Bayonne questioned, and Kane sat behind the desk. Kane leaned over and took a bottle and three glasses off the mobile bar. Bayonne asked for water, and Kane filled two glasses at the sink. Kane sipped on two fingers of vodka.

Kane said, "She's our mother, for Christ's sake. I did what I had to do. Either of you would've done the same."

Bayonne hadn't asked Adam McKenna about Molly Matches being Molly McKenna. He'd assumed they were related somehow, but he'd prioritized some fresh air and privacy over having the conversation in The Side Saddle. Kane had cut them off, and suddenly the pieces were beginning to fit.

Kane swallowed his drink and poured himself another. "I'm not mad at Dad, not anymore. I was for a long time, but now . . . . I don't know. I've seen too much. What he did was bad, but he was just so unhappy, so haunted."

Adam and Bayonne listened while Kane stumbled through a childhood Bayonne had only glimpsed through carbon impressions of sealed court records. Occasionally, Kane would pause and stare at the wall above Adam's head, as though the right words had been written there among the numbers for a good time. Kane remembered the beatings his father gave each of them in turn, beatings for little mistakes, beatings for saying something misconstrued, and beatings for no reason at all. His memory slid through fits and fragments, Adam crying through the night, Kane going to school with scars and bruises, his mother using makeup to hide Adam's bruises or her own, visiting his mother in the hospital, gluing together broken toys, and cleaning wasted dinners off the walls and cupboards. He also remembered the kiss his mother gave him, the look in her eyes, and the things she couldn't say, things he hoped she wanted to say, the night she left.

Years later, when he was in prison, he heard stories about a prostitute who couldn't talk. Guys joked about how she was the perfect woman. The woman matched his mother's description, and after Kane got out, he took the job with Bruno, so he could look for her. Kane searched the brothels, trolled the street corners and flop houses, and paid orderlies and nurses in rehab clinics, hospitals, and psych wards all over town to watch out for a woman who matched Molly's description and, if they saw her, to contact him to receive a reward. A little over a year passed when he got the call.

She'd been in the middle of the street, almost run over by the squad car that found her, and then taken to the hospital, where she'd been treated for a head injury, a broken arm, and several infections, topical and venereal. The doctors realized there were other issues, that she was an addict and probably had some minor brain damage. X-rays and a CT scan showed that, over the years, her skull had been cracked and she'd had fractures in both forearms, one wrist, one leg, and three ribs without ever receiving consistent medical attention. A psychologist worked with her and placed her in a state sponsored rehab program.

Kane visited her twice a week and paid for continued care after the state program ran its course. When she was released, he wanted her to go into a home, or at least take a job in a program where she could meet nice people, clean people, people with whom she had something in common, by which he meant people who were handicapped. She didn't want that. She wanted to work, and she claimed she didn't fit in anywhere else.

When she first moved in with Kane, he was living in a one bedroom, and for a month he slept on the couch. He wouldn't have it any other way. Her emotions ran the gamut. She had tantrums at times and appeared giddy at others. Kane would wake in the night to the sounds of her guttural, chesty moans, tears streaming down her face, or the staccato rhythm of her head thumping the wall, after he'd removed the headboard. The third week she disappeared, only to return three days later wearing the same clothes. Kane never knew where she'd been or if she'd eaten.

Kane bought The Side Saddle, so Molly would have a home, and he bought the apartment, so they could have a place to live. He'd thought, if her health improved, she might be able to run The Saddle, but it was clear, with her disabilities, she was better suited as the janitor.

"I tried to make The Saddle a place where she'd be happy. I wanted her dreams to come true. I guess I don't know what old whores dream about. I don't know why she did what she did, made the choices she made. They might've been the only choices she felt she had. Was she running away from our home or running toward a perpetual party or both? I've never known, and it never made sense to me. All I knew was that she was my mother, and I had to take care of her. I thought she liked being close to her old life but not being part of her old life, but it's like she was on the outside looking in, like she always had been. I don't know. I've never understood."

Adam spoke for the first time: "Why can't she talk?"

Kane took a drink before responding. "Don't you remember? Don't you remember anything from before? You were eight when Mom left, almost twelve when Dad died."

"I woke up in the hospital a little over a week later. I'd been drugged, and I couldn't move much. They had me bandaged up, both arms and one leg in casts. I'd had a bad concussion."

"Do you remember what happened?"

"Only what they told me."

"Do you remember any of us?"

"A little. I thought I did, but it was a long time ago. You're so different. She's so different. I remember you teasing me. I remember her face. I don't remember her not talking, but I don't remember her voice. There was a photograph of her on the stairs. They were so happy. We were all happy."

"There were good times, Adam, sure, the Christmas we made the paper ornaments and the trip to the Black Hills. Dad was proud the year your junior rec team won the city championship."

"What did Mom think? I remember her there, watching."

"She'd been gone three years by then. It might've been the last time Dad was ever happy, but Mom wasn't there."

Bayonne lit a cigarette, saw the look in Kane's eyes, handed it to him, and lit a second. Kane sucked the smoke into his lungs and slid an ashtray closer to Bayonne. "Before she left, Mom loved you best. I reminded her of Dad, but she saw herself in you, I think." A couple ticks passed while Kane stared at the wall. "They were never happy. They'd only married because Mom was pregnant. They only stayed married because they didn't know what else to do. They were Catholic. They did what people do." Kane dragged on his cigarette. "You really don't remember why she can't talk?"

"How many times do I need to say it? I don't remember. I tried to make her talk to me, for Christ's sake."

"You found her after it happened. You walked in on her after Dad did that to her. He'd been beating her, and he took the belt off her and choked her with it, choked her out and left here there on the bedroom floor. I had to get the neighbor to drive her to the hospital. Dad had squeezed her neck so hard he'd crushed her voice box."

"The hell you say." The words came out of Bayonne's throat as more of a squeak.

The statement settled over the room like a shadow, and Kane rubbed his cigarette out in the ashtray without taking his eyes off Bayonne.

The clock on the wall ticked through the tension.

"The hell I say."

"You knew."

"I suspected. I didn't know."

"I was hearing the murders. I was hearing silence, her silence. You knew, and you hid it, had me chasing my tail."

"What would you have done? She's my mother, Vince. I knew, if it was her, you'd figure it out, and that would be that. I wasn't going to turn my mother in, and I wasn't going to do your job for you."

"That can't be." Adam held his face in his hands. He leaned forward and vomited through his fingers.

"Jesus Christ," Bayonne said. "She's recreating her own trauma, recreating the way she became who she is today. The belts on the victims' necks, don't you see? She uses their belts."

"Stop talking. Both of you stop," Adam said.

"Molly Matches is the killer," Bayonne said. "She's connected to every scene. She was at Mason's and Alfie's with the girls who worked Shady Pines and The Spanish Fly.

No one suspected her because she's handicapped. Everyone looked past her. Nobody saw her as a person."

"Maybe they got what they deserved."

"What have you done, Kane? If you'd told me, we could've stopped her after the first."

"Addicts and slags, Vinnie. You can't use people and expect to get away with it. Nobody can. We all pay for our crimes. That's what life has taught me. All of us pay. Nobody died who didn't have it coming."

Kane stared into the carpet, his scar a pinkish tint, almost glowing, and his eyes clear. He leaned back in his chair, and his left hand shook the ice in his half-empty glass, brought the glass to his lips, and he drained the liquid, drawing a cube into his mouth with his tongue, sucking on the cube, and spitting it back into the glass.

"Mom would never do that," Adam said. "She's not that person."

"We've got to take her in. You know that, Kane."

"This can't be right." Adam's voice had risen in pitch.

Kane leaned forward. "You still need to prove it was her. All you've done is clarify a motive. That's not proof."

"It's enough to take her in for questioning and get a warrant to search her place, your place."

"You think you can link her to my place? You think I'm dumb enough to let you search me twice? You'll never get a warrant to search my home, Vinnie. Never again."

"She'll be charged for this, and she'll get the help she needs."

"When? After you find some evidence? After a trial? After

she's sat in general population for months? You know what they'll do to her."

"I know what we need to do."

"You need to take a deep breath and consider what you know and what you think."

"I know what she's done."

"You have no idea what she's done, what she's been through. You have no idea."

Adam leaned over the sink, started to wash his hands, and vomited a second time. The sour liquid splashed onto his shirt.

Kane and Bayonne locked eyes, both of them leaning forward. Kane had slid his hand into one of his desk drawers and gripped his Ruger. Neither knew exactly what to do, how to handle the situation. They might've figured it out, come to an agreement, a point of compromise where they both felt understood, or maybe that was a load of horseshit. They were a hair's breadth from the precipice, and they both knew it. Neither were ready to leap, but both were out of options.

"Kane, get the fuck out here!" Karla had some pipes to go with those melons.

Kane took his pistol from the drawer and walked into the bar. Bayonne and Adam followed, and the three of them clustered together at the end of the hall. None of them realized it, but what they saw meant the conversation had lost any meaning.

Molly, naked as a newborn, stood on the stairs, blood smeared across her porcelain skin and smeared through her platinum hair. She'd wiped blood on her face, drawing lines with her fingers, like a native prepared for war. She'd wiped blood on her neck, legs, and stomach using her small, almost childlike, fingers and palms. One breast had been dipped in blood, but the liquid had run and smeared. The red, already darkening to black, stood out on her butter-milk skin. Two rosy nipples pointed at her sons, accusingly, as though it was all their fault. They would occasionally wonder if it had been. She walked toward them, gnawing at the air and waving a straight razor back and forth. She stumbled, caught herself on the railing, and groaned.

Seth appeared at the top of the stairs, saw her, and moved to help or hinder. She slashed him across the chest.

Like a toddler learning to walk, she took one step at a time, first one foot and then the other, but the look in her eyes, an aged agony, spoke of years of pain, years of barriers between her and the rest of the world, years of alienation and abuse.

At the bottom of the stairs, she rushed Kane, the razor sliding in a wide arc.

Kane danced away, said, "Molly, what's happened? We can fix this. I'm here to help you. You need to put the razor down."

Molly waved the razor in a slow circle, tears streaked the blood that covered her face, and she moved her mouth as though she were silently screaming bloody murder. Was she in pain or in a rage? Nobody could tell. Nobody spoke her language, not anymore.

Adam screamed, "Mom, stop. Why are you doing this?

What is wrong with you?"

Kane crouched, his arms extended, pistol in one hand, and scanned the room. Seth lay on the stairs bleeding. Bayonne stood in the hall, both his cigarette and .38 police special pointed at the floor. Hookers and johns stared from the railing above and watched from the tables below. The performer on stage covered her mouth with her hands, the rest of her exposed to the world, but for the first time in her short career, no one watched. Karla yawned behind the bar, a cold beer in one hand and a cigarette in the other. She might've been at this job too long.

Molly raised the razor above her head and took a step toward Adam. Adam fell to his knees. Molly paused in front of her youngest son. She groaned from the depths of her chest and swung the razor in a long arc. Adam tilted his head back, closed his eyes, and kept his hands on the floor near his knees, palms facing the ceiling.

Kane stepped forward and shot his mother through the ear.

Someone had stopped the music, and everyone stared at the corpse of the handicapped janitor.

Kane knelt over his mother's body and spoke in a whisper. "The men who did this to you are dead. They'll never hurt anyone again. Before you're in the ground, I'll watch The Dungeon burn."

Kane stood, slid his pistol into the back of his pants, and said, "There. She's out of her misery."

"I didn't see that coming," Karla said from behind the bar. "Shit."

One of the girls called from the top of the stairs, "Kane, there's more up here."

Kane spoke to the room: "None of you saw this. You didn't see a thing. You were never here."

As though a strong man, a man in charge, could say that and make it all go away.

He turned to Karla. "Get everyone out of here. Close up for the night."

She nodded and took a sip of her beer.

"Do it now."

Seth stood, one hand covering the wound across his chest.

"You heard the man. Everyone move, please. Get your things and go home. There is nothing to see here."

Kane and Bayonne followed the trail of blood and found Diamond Molloy in one of the rooms, sliced across the belly and pried open like a biological inkwell. A needle lay on the floor, and her throat had been cut from ear to ear. On the wall, Molly had written them all a message in blood.

Hush Little Baby

Don't Say A Word

In the janitor's closet, Bayonne found the heroin she'd been giving them. Days later, when he got the results back from the lab, he would learn it had been laced with a tranquilizer, and he would match the tranquilizer to each victim's toxicology.

"She gave them the dope that knocked them out, then strangled them. She's the killer, without a doubt. Christ,

Kane. I don't know what to say."

"You cracked your case. There won't be a trial. Just keep her real last name and any connection to me or Adam out of the papers."

"Sure, Kane. That's the least I can do. Are you going to be okay?"

"Don't worry about it."

Bayonne stared at the side of his face. What do you say to that?

Kane cleared his throat, and said, "Anyway, in a weird way, this all seems reasonable."

"How do you figure?"

"My problems were always going to be my problems, whether they were my doing or not. I couldn't expect somebody else to solve them, or for them to take care of themselves. I either had to handle things myself, getting my hands dirty, or spend my life running like Molly did. Those were always my only choices."

Adam had been standing, forgotten, in the doorway. He'd been in such a daze he hadn't said a word. When he screamed, Bayonne and Kane jumped.

The scream lingered, and Bayonne was still hearing it when Adam pushed Kane. Kane caught him in his arms, spun him around, and dropped him onto the floor. Like his mother had an hour before, Adam rolled over onto all fours, ready to pounce.

"You don't care. You never cared," Adam said. "You took everything from me. Everything. You ruined our home. Now you've killed both our parents. For what? These weren't only your problems. These weren't *your* choices to make. Who are you? What is wrong with you?"

"I didn't kill our parents, Adam. I killed our mother. You killed our father."

"What? I read the police report. You went to St. Catherine's. Everyone knows you killed him."

"Nobody knows what everybody knows. I was never found guilty. I just never fought the charges. The court considered it self-defense. Father Nick petitioned the court to make me a ward of the church rather than placing me in foster care. I thought you were dead and I was alone in the world. I didn't see any reason to try to explain things." Kane shrugged. "Why fight it?"

"I didn't . . . . What?"

"You did. We were both struggling with him. You were grabbing at the things on his belt, got his gun out of its holster, and shot him through the femoral artery. He bled out in a few seconds."

"No. That's not true."

"Adam, this is who they were. Our father was a bully, and our mother a child. Dad was wasted when you shot him, a blood alcohol content over .25. That's the way he was, never in control. He was so angry, so filled with rage and pain. He would've killed you. He probably would've killed me. He killed our mother when he took her voice. You were protecting yourself. You had to."

Adam leaned back, the drying blood on the floor stuck to and stained his hands and knees.

"By the time I found Mom, she wasn't our mother anymore. She was a shell of who she'd been. She'd become something else, someone haunted by her past, things she'd done, and things done to her. I didn't realize she was as bad as all this, but I knew she had issues I didn't understand. I did the best I could, but she just wasn't all there."

"I never knew her. I didn't even know she couldn't talk."

"I hardly knew her, either. She couldn't tell anyone who she was. She was gone eighteen years ago, maybe even before that. There's no changing things."

Adam sat in a pool of blood and cried.

Bayonne was on his way out to use the phone when Kane said, "It's not your fault. It's not my fault. It's not our fault."

Bayonne paused in the doorway and watched the two of them, neither looking directly at the other.

"This was never about us. This is just the way things were, and we need to learn to live with it. We need to learn to live a different way."

Printed in Great Britain
by Amazon